The Destiny of
Nathalie X
and Other Stories

WILLIAM BOYD

The Destiny of
Nathalie X
and Other Stories

ALFRED A. KNOPF   NEW YORK   1997

THIS IS A BORZOI BOOK
PUBLISHED BY ALFRED A. KNOPF

Copyright © 1995, 1997 by William Boyd

All rights reserved under International and Pan-American Copyright Conventions. Published in the United States by Alfred A. Knopf, Inc., New York. Distributed by Random House, Inc., New York. Originally published in Great Britain, in different form, by Sinclair-Stevenson, London, in 1995.

http://www.randomhouse.com/

Library of Congress Cataloging-in-Publication Data

Boyd, William.
    The destiny of Nathalie X and other stories /
William Boyd.—
    1st ed.
      p. cm.
    ISBN 0-679-44705-9
    1. Manners and customs—Fiction.   I. Title.
PR6052.09192D47   1997
823'.914–dc20   96-17564
              CIP

Manufactured in the United States of America
First American Edition

For Susan

CONTENTS

AUTHOR'S NOTE

Four of these stories have been published in *Granta:* "The Destiny of Nathalie X," "Cork," "Transfigured Night" and "Alpes-Maritimes." "Alpes-Maritimes" also made it into a second Penguin edition of my first volume of short stories—*On the Yankee Station* (1981)—but has never been collected between hard covers and I wanted to include it here, albeit in a slightly altered form. "Loose Continuity" was published in *The New Yorker*, "The Dream Lover" in *London Magazine*, "Hôtel des Voyageurs" in the *Daily Telegraph* and "N Is for N" appeared in *Hockney's Alphabet* (Faber and Faber, 1993).

WB
London, 1997

The Destiny of
Nathalie X
and Other Stories

The Destiny of
Nathalie X

Man's Voice (over)

I ONCE HEARD a theory about this town, this place where
we work and wrangle, where we swindle and swive. It was
told to me by this writer I knew. He said: "It's only a
dance, but then again, it's the only dance." I'm not so sure he's
right, but anyway, he's dead now . . .

Fade In

ONCE UPON a time—actually, not so very long ago at all,
come to think of it—in east-central West Africa, on one ener-
vating May morning, Aurélien No sat on the stoop of his father's house staring aimlessly at the road that led to Murkina
Leto, state capital of the People's Republic of Kiq. The sun's
force seemed to press upon the dusty brown landscape with
redundant intensity, Aurélien thought idly, there was no
moisture left out there to evaporate and it seemed . . . He
searched for a word for a second or two: it seemed "stupid"
that all that calorific energy should go to waste.

He called for his little brother Marius to fetch him another beer but no reply came from inside the house. He scratched his cheek; he thought he could taste metal in his mouth—that new filling. He shifted his weight on his cane chair and wondered vaguely why cane made that curious squeaking sound. Then his eye was caught by the sight of a small blue van that was making its way up the middle of the road with what seemed like undue celerity, tooting its horn at the occasional roadside pedestrian and browsing cow not so much to scare them out of the way as to announce the importance of this errand it was on.

To Aurélien's mild astonishment the blue van turned abruptly into his father's driveway and stopped equally abruptly before the front door. As the laterite dust thrown up by the tires slowly dispersed, the postman emerged from the auburn cloud like a messenger from the gods carrying before him a stiff envelope blazoned with an important-looking crest.

MARIUS NO. For sure, I remember that day when he won the prize. Personally, I was glad of the distraction. He had been emmerding me all morning. "Get this," "Get that," "Fetch me a beer." I just knew it had gone quiet for ten minutes. When I came out onto the stoop he was sitting there, looking even more vacant than normal, just staring at this paper in his hands. "Hey, Coco," I said to him. "Military service, mmm? Poor *salaud*. Wait till those bastard sergeants give you one up the *cul*." He said nothing, so I took the paper from his hands and read it. It was the hundred thousand francs that had shocked him, struck him dumb.

When *Le Destin de Nathalie X* (metteur en scène Aurélien No) won the Prix d'Or at the *concours général* in Paris of l'Ecole

Supérieure des Etudes Cinématographiques (ESEC), the Kiq minister of culture (Aurélien's brother-in-law) laid on a reception for two hundred guests at the ministry. After a long speech the minister called Aurélien onto the podium to shake his hand. Aurélien had gathered his small tight dreadlocks into a loose sheaf on the top of his head, and the photographs from that special evening show him startled and blinking in a silvery wash of the flashbulbs, some natural flinch causing the fronds of his dreadlock sheaf to toss simultaneously in one direction as if blown by a stiff breeze.

The minister asked him what he planned to do with the prize money.

"Good question," Aurélien said, and thought for ten seconds or so before replying. "It's a condition of the prize that I put the money toward another film."

"Here in Kiq?" the minister said, smiling knowingly.

"Of course."

DELPHINE DRELLE. "It's impossible," I said when he called me. "Completely out of the question. Are you mad? What kind of film could you make in Kiq?" He came to my apartment in Paris, he said he wanted me to be in his new film. I say I don't want to be an actress. Well, as soon as I started explaining Aurélien saw I was making sense. That's what I like about Aurélien, by the way, he is responsive to the powers of reason. Absolutely not, I said to Aurélien, never in my life. He said he had an idea, but only I could do it. I said, look what happened the last time, do you think I'm crazy? I've only been out of the clinic one month. He just smiled at me. He said, what do you think if we go to Hollywood?

Aurélien No turned out of the rental park at LAX and wondered which direction to take. Delphine Drelle sat beside him studying her face intently in the mirror of her compact and moaning about the dehydrating effect of international air travel. In the back seat of the car sat Bertrand Holbish, a photographer, and ex-boyfriend of Delphine, squashed in the cramped space left by the two large scratched and dented silver aluminum boxes that held the camera and the sound equipment.

Aurélien turned left, drove four hundred meters and turned left again. He saw a sign directing him to the freeway and followed it until he reached a hotel. DOLLARWIZE INN, he saw it was called as he pulled carefully into the forecourt. The hotel was a six-story rectangle. The orange plastic cladding on the balconies had been bleached salmon pink by the sun.

"Here we are," Aurélien said. "This is perfect."

"Where's Hollywood?" Bertrand Holbish asked.

"Can't be far away," Aurélien said.

BERTRAND HOLBISH. Immediately, when he asked me, I said to Aurélien that I didn't know much about sound. He said you switch it on, you point the volume. No, you check the volume and you point the, ah, what's the word? . . . What? Ah yes, "boom." I said: You pay my ticket? You buy me drugs? He said of course, only don't touch Delphine. [Laughs, coughs] That's Aurélien for you, one crazy guy.

DELPHINE DRELLE. Did I tell you that he is a very attractive man, Aurélien? Yes? He's a real African, you know, strong face, strong African face . . . and his lips, they're like they're carved. He's tall, slim. He has this hair, it's like that tennis player, Noah, like little braids hanging down over his forehead. Sometimes he puts beads on the end of them. I don't like it so much. I want him to shave his head. Completely. He speaks real good English, Aurélien. I never knew this about him. I asked him once how he pronounced his name and he said something like "Ngoh." He says it is a common name in Kiq. But everybody pronounces it differently. He doesn't mind.

When Aurélien went out the next day to scout for locations, he discovered that the area they were staying in was called Westchester. He drove through the featureless streets—unusually wide, he thought, for such an inactive neighborhood—the air charged and thunderous with landing jetliners, until he found a small cluster of shops beneath a revolving sign declaiming BROGAN'S MINI-MALL. There was a deli, a pharmacy, a novelty store, a Korean grocery and a pizzeria-cum-coffee-shop that had most of the features he was looking for: half a dozen tables on the sidewalk, a predominantly male staff, a license to sell alcoholic beverages. He went inside, ordered a cappuccino and asked how long they stayed open in the evenings. Late, came the answer. For the first time since he had suggested coming to Los Angeles Aurélien sensed a small tremor of excitement. Perhaps it would be possible after all. He looked at the expressionless tawny faces of the men behind the counter and the cheerful youths serving food and drink. He felt sure these gentlemen would allow him to film in their establishment—for a modest fee, of course.

MICHAEL SCOTT GEHN. Have you ever seen *Le Destin de Nathalie X*? Extraordinary film, extraordinary. No, I tell you, I'd put it right up there with *Un Chien andalou*, J. J. Todd's *Last Walk*, *The Chelsea Girls*, Downey's *Chafed Elbows*. That category of film. Surreal, bizarre . . . Let's not beat about the bush, sometimes downright incomprehensible, but it gets to you. Somehow, subcutaneously. You know, I spend more time thinking about certain scenes in *Nathalie X* than I do about Warner's annual slate. And it's my business, what more can I say? Do you smoke? Do you have any nonviolent objections if I do? Thank you, you're very gracious. I'm not kidding, you can't be too careful here. *Nathalie X . . .* OK. It's very simple and outstandingly clever. A girl wakes up in her bed in her room—

Aurélien looked at his map. Delphine and Bertrand stood at his shoulder, sunglassed, fractious.

"We have to go from here . . . to here."

"Aurélien, when are we going to film?"

"Tomorrow. Maybe. First we walk it through."

Delphine let her shoulders slump. "But we have the stock. Why don't we start?"

"I don't know. I need an idea. Let's walk it through."

He took Bertrand's elbow and guided him across the road to the other side. He made half a square with his thumbs and his forefingers and framed Delphine in it as she lounged against the exit sign of the Dollarwize Inn.

"Turn right," Aurélien shouted across the road. "I'll tell you which way to go."

MICHAEL SCOTT GEHN. —A girl wakes up in her own bed in her own room, somewhere in Paris. She gets out of bed and puts on her makeup, very slowly, very deliberately. No score, just the noises she makes as she goes about her business. You know, paints her nails, mascara on eyelashes. She hums a bit, she starts to sing a song to herself, snatches of a song in English. Beatles song, from the "White Album," what's it called? Oh yeah: "Rocky Raccoon." This girl's French, right, and she's singing in English with a French accent, just quietly to herself. The song sounds totally different. Totally. Extraordinary effect. Bodywide goose bumps. This takes about twenty, thirty minutes. You are completely, but *completely*, held. You do not notice the time passing. That something so totally—let's not beat about the bush—banal, can hold you that way. Extraordinary. We're talking mundanity, here, absolute diurnal minutiae. I see, what, two hundred and fifty movies a year in my business, not counting TV. I am replete with film. Sated. But I am held. No, mesmerized would be fair. [Pause] Did I tell you the girl was naked?

"Turn left," Aurélien called.

Delphine obliged and walked past the mirror glass façade of an office building.

"Stop."

Aurélien made a note on the map and turned to Bertrand.

"What could she do here, Bertrand? She needs to do something."

"I don't know. How should I know?"

"Something makes her stop."

"She could step in some dogshit."

Aurélien reflected for a while. He looked around him: at the cracked parched concrete of the street, the dusty burnish on the few parked cars. There was a bleached, fumy quality to the light that day, a softened glare that hurt the eyes. The air reverberated as another jumbo hauled itself out of LAX.

"Not a bad idea," he said. "Thanks, Bertrand." He called to Delphine. "OK, go up to the end of the road and turn left."

MICHAEL SCOTT GEHN. I've written a lot about this movie, analyzed the hell out of it, the way it's shot, the way it manipulates mood, but it only struck me the other day how it works. Essentially, basically. It's all in the title, you see. *Le Destin.* "The Destiny of Nathalie X." Destiny. What does destiny have in store for this girl, I should say, this astoundingly attractive girl? She gets up, she puts on her makeup, she sings a song, she gets dressed. She leaves her apartment building and walks through the streets of Paris to a café. It's nighttime. She sits in this café and orders a beer. We're watching her, we're waiting. She drinks more beers, she seems to be getting drunk. People come and go. We wait. We wonder. What is the destiny of Nathalie X? (It's pronounced "Eeeks" in French. Not "Ecks," "Eeeks.") And then? But I don't want to spoil the movie for you.

They started filming on their sixth day in Los Angeles. It was late afternoon—almost magic hour—and the orange sun basted the city in a thick viscous light. Aurélien shot the sequence of the walk in front of the mirror glass building. The moving cloudscape on the mirror glass curtain wall was disturbingly beautiful. Aurélien had a moment's regret that he was filming in black and white.

Delphine wore a short black skirt and a loose, V-neck taupe cashmere sweater (no bra). On her feet she wore skin-colored kid loafers, so fine you could roll them into a ball. She had a fringed suede bag over her shoulder. Her long hair was dyed a light sandy blond and—after much debate—was down.

Aurélien set up the camera across the road for the first take. Bertrand stood beside him and pointed his microphone in the general direction of Delphine.

Aurélien switched on the camera, chalked scene one on the clapper board, walked into the frame, clicked it and said, *"Vas y, Delphine."*

Nathalie X walked along the sidewalk. When she reached the middle of the mirror glass she stopped. She took off one of her shoes and peeled the coin of chewing gum from its sole. She stuck the gum to the glass wall, refitted her shoe and walked on.

MICHAEL SCOTT GEHN. I have to say as a gesture of contempt for Western materialism, the capitalist macrostructure that we function in, that takes some beating. And it's not in the French version. Aurélien No has been six days in Los Angeles and he comes up with something as succinct, as moodily epiphanic as that. That's what I call talent. Not raw talent, talent of the highest sophistication.

BERTRAND HOLBISH. The way Delphine cut her hair, you know, is the clue, I think. It's blond, right? Long and she has a fringe, OK? But not like anybody else's fringe. It's just too long. It hangs to her lower eyelash. To here [gestures], to the middle of her nose. So she shakes her head all the time to clear her vision a little. She pulls it aside—like this—with one finger when she wants to see something a little better . . . You know, many many people look at Delphine and find this very exciting, sexually, I mean. She's a pretty girl, for sure, nice body, nice face. But I see these girls everywhere. Especially in Los Angeles. It's something about this fringe business that makes her different. People look at her all the time. When we were waiting for Aurélien we—Delphine and me—used to play backgammon. For hours. The fringe, hanging there, over her eyes. It drove me fucking crazy. I offered her five hundred dollars to cut it one centimeter, just one centimeter. She refused. She knew, Delphine, she knew.

Aurélien filmed the walk to the café first. It took four days, starting late afternoon, always approaching the café at dusk. He filmed Nathalie's *levée* in one sustained twelve-hour burst. Delphine woke, made up, sang and dressed eight times that day in a series of long takes, cuts only coming when the film ran out. The song changed: Delphine sang Bob Dylan's "She Belongs to Me" with the pronoun changed to "He." This was Delphine's idea, and a good one Aurélien thought, the only problem was she kept forgetting. "He's an artist, she don't look back," Delphine sang in her flat breathy voice as she combed her hair, "He never stumbles, she's got no place to fall."

Every evening they would go to the pizzeria and eat. Aurélien insisted that Delphine get drunk, not knee-walking drunk, but as far as woozy inebriation. Of course the waiters came to know them and conversation ensued. "What you guys doin' here anyway? Making a movie? Great. Another beer for the lady? No problemo."

After a week's regular visiting Aurélien asked the owner, a small nervy man called George Malinverno, if they could film at the pizzeria, outside on the "terrace," for one night only. They agreed on a remuneration of two hundred dollars.

MICHAEL SCOTT GEHN. Have you ever heard of the Topeka Film Festival? That's Topeka, Kansas? No? Neither have I. So you can understand that I was kind of pissed when my editor assigned me to cover it. It ran a week, the theme was "Kansas in the Western, 1970–1980." It's not my subject, my last book was on Murnau, for Christ's sake, but let's not get embroiled in office politics. The point is I'm on my way to the airport and I realize I've left my razor and shaving foam behind. I pull into this mini-mall where there's a pharmacy. I'm coming out of the shop and I see there's a film crew setting up a shot of the pizzeria. Normally I see a film crew and chronic catatonia sets in. But there's something about this one: the guy holding the boom mike looks like he's stoned— even I can see that it keeps dropping into the shot. So I wander over. The camera is set up behind these plants, kind of poking through a gap, like it's hidden or something. And there's this black guy behind the camera with this great hair with beads on it. I see he's D.P. and clapper boy and director. He calls out into the darkness and this sensational-looking girl walks into the pizzeria terrace thing. She sits down and orders a beer and they just keep filming. After about two minutes the soundman drops the boom and they have to start over. I hear them talking—French. I couldn't believe it. I had this guy figured for some wannabe homeboy director out of South Central LA. But they're talking French to each other. When was the last time a French crew shot a movie in this town? I introduced myself and that's when he told me about *Nathalie X* and the Prix d'Or. I bought them all some drinks and he told me his story and gave me a videocassette of the movie. Fuck Topeka, I thought, I knew this was too good to miss. French underground movies shooting next door to LAX. Are you kidding me? They were all staying in some fleabag motel under the flight path, for God's sake. I called my editor and threatened to take the feature to *American Film*. He reassigned me.

The night's shooting at the pizzeria did not go well. Bertrand proved incapable of holding the boom aloft for more than two minutes and this was one sequence where Aurélien knew he needed sound. He spent half an hour taping a mike under Delphine's table and snaking the wires around behind the potted plants. Then this man who said he was a film critic turned up and offered to buy them a drink. When Aurélien was talking to him, Delphine drank three margaritas and a negroni. When they tried to restart, her reflexes had slowed to such an extent that when she remembered she had to throw the glass of beer, the waiter had turned away and she missed completely. Aurélien wrapped it up for the night. Holbish wandered off and Aurélien drove Delphine back to the hotel. She was sick in the parking lot and started to cry and that's when Aurélien thought about the gun.

KAISER PREVOST. I rarely read *film/e*. It's way too pretentious. Ditto that creep Michael Scott Gehn. Any guy with three names and I get irrationally angry. What's wrong with plain old Michael Gehn? Are there so many Michael Gehns out there that he has to distinguish himself? "Oh, you mean Michael *Scott* Gehn, I got you now." I'd like a Teacher's, straight up, with three ice cubes. Three. Thank you. Anyway, for some reason I bought it that week—it was the issue with that great shot of Jessica, no, Lanier on the cover—and I read the piece about this French director Aurélien No and this remake *Seeing Through Nathalie* he was shooting in town. Gehn—sorry, Michael Scott Gehn—is going on like this guy is sitting there holding God's hand and I read about the Prix d'Or and this *Nathalie X* film and I think, hmmm, has Aurélien got representation? This is Haig. This is not Teacher's.

MICHAEL SCOTT GEHN. I knew, I just knew when this young guy Kaiser Prevost calls me up, things would change. "Hi, Michael," he says. "Kaiser Prevost here." I don't know jack shit about any Kaiser Prevost but I do know I hate it when someone uses my Christian name from the get-go—what's wrong with Mr. Gehn? Also his tone just assumes, just oozes the assumption that I'm going to know who he is. I mean, I am a film critic of some reputation, if I may be immodest for a moment, and these young guys in the agencies . . . There's a problem of perspectives, that's what it comes down to, that's what bedevils us. I have a theory about this town: there is no overview, nobody steps back, no one stands on the mountain looking down on the valley. Imagine an army composed entirely of officers. Let me put it another way: imagine an army where everyone *thinks* they're an officer. That's Hollywood, that's the film business. No one wants to accept the hierarchy, no one will admit they are a foot soldier. And I'm sorry, a young agent in a boutique agency is just a G.I. Joe to me. Still, he was a persuasive fellow and he had some astute and flattering things to say about the article. I told him where Aurélien was staying.

Aurélien No met Kaiser Prevost for breakfast in the coffee shop of the Dollarwize. Prevost looked around him as if he had just emerged from some prolonged comatose sleep.

"You know, I've lived in this town for all my life and I don't think I've ever even driven through here. And as for shooting a movie . . . It's a first!"

"Well, it was right for me."

"Oh no. I appreciate that. I think it's fresh, original. Gehn certainly thinks a lot of you."

"Who?"

Prevost showed him the article in *film/e*. Aurélien flicked through it. "He has written a lot."

"Have you got a rough assembly of the new movie? Anything I could see?"

"No."

"Any dailies? Maybe you call them rushes."

"There are no dailies on this film. None of us see anything until it is finished."

"The ultimate auteur, huh? That is impressive. More than that, it's cool."

Aurélien chuckled. "No, it's a question of—what do you say?—*faute de mieux*."

"I couldn't have put it better myself. Look, Aurélien, I'd like you to meet somebody, a friend of mine at a studio. Can I fix that up? I think it would be mutually beneficial."

"Sure. If you like."

KAISER PREVOST. I have a theory about this town, this place, about the way it works: it operates best when people go beyond the bounds of acceptable behavior. You reach a position, a course of action suggests itself, and you say, "This makes me morally uncomfortable," or "This will constitute a betrayal of friendship." In any other walk of life you withdraw, you rethink. But my theory instead goes like this: make it your working maxim. *When you find yourself in a position of normative doubt, then that is the sign to commit.* My variation on this theory is that the really successful people go one step further. They find themselves in this moral gray area, they move right on into the black. Look at Vincent Bandine.

I knew I was doing the right thing with Aurélien No because I had determined not to tell my boss. Sheldon started ArtFocus after ten years at ICM. It was going well but it's clear that the foundations are giving. Two months ago we lost Larry Swiftsure. Last Saturday I get a call from Sheldon: Donata Vail has walked to CAA. His own Donata. He was weeping and was looking for consolation, which I hope I provided. Under these circumstances it seemed to me at best morally dubious that I should go behind his back and try to set up a deal for Aurélien at Alcazar. I was confident it was the only route to take.

The gun idea persisted, it nagged at Aurélien. He talked about it with Bertrand, who thought it was an amusing notion.

"A gun, why not? Pam-pam-pam-pam."

"Could you get me one? A handgun?" Aurélien asked. "Maybe one of those guys you know . . ."

"A prop gun? Or a real one?"

"Oh, I think it should be real. Don't tell Delphine, though."

The next day Bertrand showed Aurélien a small scarred automatic. It cost five hundred dollars. Aurélien did not question him about its provenance.

He reshot the end of Nathalie's *levée*. Nathalie, dressed, is about to leave her room, her hand is on the doorknob. She pauses, turns and goes to a dresser, from whose top drawer she removes the gun. She checks the clip and places it in her fringed suede shoulder bag. She leaves.

He and Delphine had a prolonged debate about whether they should reshoot the entire walk to the restaurant. Delphine thought it was pointless. How, she argued, would the audience know if the gun was in her shoulder bag or not? But *you* would know, Aurélien countered, and everything might change. Delphine maintained that she would walk the same way whether she had a gun in her bag or not; also they had been in Los Angeles for three weeks and she was growing bored; *Le Destin* had been filmed in five days. A compromise was agreed: they would only reshoot the pizzeria sequence. Aurélien went off to negotiate another night's filming.

BOB BERGER. I hate to admit it but I was grateful to Kaiser Prevost when he brought the *Nathalie X* project to me. As I told him, I had admired Aurélien No's work for some years and was excited and honored at the possibility of setting up his first English-language film. More to the point, the last two films I exec'd at Alcazar had done me no favors: *Disintegrator* had only grossed 13 before they stopped tracking and *Sophomore Nite II* had gone straight to video. I liked the idea of doing something with more art quality and with a European kind of angle. I asked Kaiser to get a script to me soonest and I raised the project at our Monday morning staff meeting. I said I thought it would be a perfect vehicle for Lanier Cross. Boy, did that make Vincent sit up. Dirty old toad (he's my uncle).

KAISER PREVOST. I'll tell you one fact about Vincent Bandine. He has the cleanest teeth and the healthiest gums in Hollywood. Every morning a dental nurse comes to his house and flosses and cleans his teeth for him. Every morning, 365 days a year. That's what I call class. Have you any idea how much that must cost?

Kaiser Prevost thought he detected an unsettled quality about Aurélien as he drove him to the meeting at Alcazar. Aurélien was frowning as he looked about him. The day was perfect, the air clear, the colors ideally bright; more than that, he was going to a deal meeting at a major minor studio, or minor major depending on who you were talking to. Usually in these cases the anticipation in the car would be heady, palpable. Aurélien just made clicking noises in his mouth and fiddled with the beads on the end of his dreadlocks. Prevost told him about Alcazar Films, their money base, their ten-picture slate, their deals or potential deals with Goldie, Franklin Dean, Joel, Demi, Carlo Sancarlo and ItalFilm. The names seemed to make no impact.

As they turned up Coldwater to go over into the valley Prevost finally had to ask if everything was all right.

"There's a slight problem," Aurélien admitted. "Delphine has left."

"That's too bad," Prevost said, trying to keep the excitement out of his voice. "Gone back to France?"

"I don't know. She's left with Bertrand."

"Bitch, man."

"We still have the whole last scene to reshoot."

"Listen, Aurélien, relax. One thing you learn about working in this town. Everything can be fixed. Everything."

"How can I finish without Delphine?"

"Have you ever heard of Lanier Cross?"

VINCENT BANDINE. My nephew has two sterling qualities: he's dumb and he's eager to please. He's a good-looking kid too and that helps, no doubt about it. Sometimes, sometimes, he gets it right. Sometimes he has a sense for the popular mood. When he started talking about this "Destiny of Nathalie" film I thought he was way out of his depth until he mentioned the fact that Lanier Cross would be buck naked for the first thirty minutes. I said get the French guy in, tie him up, get him together with Lanier. She'll go for that. She'll go for the French part. If the No fellow won't play, get the Englishman in, what's his name, Tim Pascal, he'll do it. He'll do anything I tell him.

I have a theory about this town: there's too much respect for art. That's where we make all our mistakes, all of them. But if that's a given, then I'm prepared to work with it once in a while. Especially if it'll get me Lanier Cross nekkid.

MICHAEL SCOTT GEHN. When I heard that Aurélien No was doing a deal with Vincent Bandine at Alcazar, I was both suicidal and oddly proud. If you'd asked me where was the worst home possible for a remake of *Nathalie X*, I'd have said Alcazar straight off. But that's what heartens me about this burg, this place we fret and fight in. I have a theory about this town: they all talk about the "business," the "industry," how hard-nosed and bottom-line-obsessed they are, but it's not true. Or rather not the whole truth. Films of worth are made and I respect the place for it. God, I even respected Vincent Bandine for it and I never thought those words would ever issue from my mouth. We shouldn't say: look at all the crap that gets churned out, instead we should be amazed at the good films that do emerge from time to time. There is a heart here and it's still beating even though the pulse is kind of thready.

Aurélien was impressed with the brutal economy of Bob Berger's office. A black ebony desk sat in the middle of a charcoal gray carpet. Two large black leather sofas were separated by a thick sheet of glass resting on three sharp cones. On one wall were two black and white photographs of lily trumpets and on another was an African mask. There was no evidence of work or the tools of work apart from the long, flattened telephone on his desk. Berger himself was wearing crushed banana linen, he was in his mid-twenties, tall and deeply tanned.

Berger shook Aurélien's hand warmly, his left hand gripping Aurélien's forearm firmly as if he were a drowning man about to be hauled from a watery grave. He drew Aurélien to one of the leather sofas and sat him upon it. Prevost slid down beside him. A great variety of drinks were offered though Aurélien's choice of beer caused some consternation. Berger's assistant was dispatched in search of one. Prevost and Berger's decaf espressos arrived promptly.

Prevost gestured at the mask. "Home sweet home, eh, Aurélien?"

"Excuse me?"

"I love African art," Berger said. "What part of Africa are you from?"

"Kiq."

"Right," Berger said.

There was a short silence.

"Oh. Congratulations," Berger said.

"Excuse me?"

"On the prize. Prix d'Or. Well deserved. Kaiser, have we got a print of *Nathalie X*?"

"We're shipping it over from Paris. It'll be here tomorrow."

"It will?" Aurélien said, a little bemused.

"Everything can be fixed, Aurélien."

"I want Lanier to see it. And Vincent."

"Bob, I don't know if it's really Vincent's scene."

"He has to see it. OK, after we sign Lanier."

"I think that would be wise, Bob."

"I want to see it again, I must say. Extraordinary piece."

"You've seen it?" Aurélien said.

"Yeah. At Cannes, I think. Or possibly Berlin. Have we got a script yet, Kaiser?"

"There is no script. Extant."

"We've got to get a synopsis. A treatment at least. Mike'll want to see something on paper. He'll never let Lanier go otherwise."

"Shit. We need a goddamn writer, then," Prevost said.

"Davide?" Berger said into the speakerphone. "We need a writer. Get Matt Friedrich." He turned to Aurélien. "You'll like him. One of the old school. What?" He listened to the phone again and sighed. "Aurélien, we're having some trouble tracking down your beer. What do you say to a Dr Pepper?"

BOB BERGER. I have a theory about this town, this place. You have people in powerful executive positions who are, to put it kindly, very ordinary-looking types. I'm not talking about intellect, I'm talking about looks. The problem is these ordinary-looking people control the lives of individuals with sensational genetic advantages. That's an unbelievably volatile mix, I can tell you. And it cuts both ways; it can be very uncomfortable. It's fine for me, I'm a handsome guy, I'm in good shape. But for most of my colleagues . . . It's the source of many of our problems. That's why I took up golf.

LANIER CROSS. Tolstoy said: "Life is a *tartine de merde* that we are obliged to consume daily."

"This is for me?" Aurélien said, looking at the house, its landscaped, multileveled sprawl, the wide maw of its vast garage.

"You can't stay down by the airport," Prevost said. "Not anymore. You can shoot in Westchester but you can't live there."

A young woman emerged from the front door. She had short chestnut hair, a wide white smile and was wearing a spandex leotard and heavy climbing boots.

"This is Nancy, your assistant."

"Hi. Good to meet you, Aurélien. Did I say that right?"

"Aurélien."

"Aurélien?"

"It's not important."

"The office is in back of the tennis court. It's in good shape."

"Look, I got to fly, Aurélien. You're meeting Lanier Cross 7:30 a.m. at the Hamburger Heaven on the Shore. Nancy'll fix everything up."

To his surprise Kaiser Prevost then embraced him. When they broke apart Aurélien thought he saw tears in his eyes.

"We'll fucking show them, man, we'll fucking show them. Onward and upward, way to fucking go."

"Any news of Delphine?"

"Who? No. Nothing yet. Any problems, call me, Aurélien. Twenty-four hours a day."

MATT FRIEDRICH. *Le Destin de Nathalie X* was not as boring as I had expected, but then I was expecting terminal boredom. I was bored, sure, but it was nice to see Paris again. That's the great thing they've got going for them, French films, they carry this wonderful cargo of nostalgic Francophilia for all non-French audiences. Pretty girl too, easy on the eye. I never thought I could happily watch a girl drink herself drunk in a French café, but I did. It was not a wasted hour and a half.

It sure freaked out Prevost and Berger, though. "Extraordinary," Prevost said, clearly moved, "extraordinary piece." Berger mused awhile before announcing, "That girl is a fox." "Michael Scott Gehn thinks it's a masterpiece," I said. They agreed, vehemently. It's one of my tricks: when you don't know what to say, when you hated it or you're really stuck and anything qualified won't pass muster, use someone else's praise. Make it up if you have to. It's infallible, I promise.

I asked them how long they wanted the synopsis to be: sentence length or half a page. Berger said it had to be over forty pages, closely spaced, so people would be reluctant to read it. "We already have coverage," he said, "but we need a document." "Make it as surreal and weird as you like," Prevost said, handing me the videocassette. "That's the whole point."

We walked out into the Alcazar lot and went in search of our automobiles. "When's he meeting Lanier?" Berger said. "Tomorrow morning. She'll love him, Bob," Prevost said. "It's a done deal." Berger gestured at the heavens. "Bountiful Jehovah," he said. "Get me Lanier."

I looked at these two guys, young enough to be my sons, as they crouched into their sleek, haunchy cars under a tallow moon, fantasizing loudly, belligerently, about this notional film, the deals, the stars, and I felt enormous pity for them. I have a theory about this town: our trouble is we are at once the most confident and the most insecure people in the world. We seem bulging with self-assurance, full of loud-voiced swagger, but in reality we're terrified, or we hate ourselves, or we're all taking happy pills of some order or another, or seeing shrinks, or getting counseled by fakirs and shamans, or fleeced by a whole gallimaufry of frauds and mountebanks. This is the Faustian pact—or should I say this is the Faust deal—you have to make in order to live and work here: you get it all, sure, but you get royally fucked up in the process. That's the price you pay. It's in the contract.

Aurélien No was directed to Lanier Cross's table in the dark rear angles of the Hamburger Heaven. Another man and a woman were sitting with her. Aurélien shook her thin hand.

She was beautiful, he saw, but so small, a child-woman, the musculature of a twelve-year-old with the sexual features of an adult.

She introduced the others, an amiable, grinning, broad-shouldered youngster and a lean crop-haired woman in her forties with a fierce strong face.

"This is my husband," she said. "Kit Vermeer. And this is Naomi Tashourian. She's a writer we work with."

"We love your work," Kit said.

"Beautiful film," echoed Lanier.

"You've seen it?" Aurélien said.

"We saw it two hours ago," Lanier said.

Aurélien looked at his watch: Nancy had made sure he was punctual—7:30 a.m.

"I called Berger, said I had to see it before we met."

"We tend to sleep in the day," Kit said. "Like bats."

"Like lemurs," Lanier said. "I don't like bats."

"Like lemurs."

"It's a beautiful film," Lanier said. "That's why we wanted to meet with you." She reached up and unfastened a large plastic bulldog clip on the top of her head and uncoiled a great dark glossy hank of hair a yard long. She pulled and tightened it, screwing it up, winding it around her right hand, piling it back on the top of her head before she refastened it in position with the clip. Everyone remained silent during this operation.

"That's why we wanted you to meet Naomi."

"This is a remake, right?" Naomi said.

"Yes. I think so."

"Excellent," Lanier said. "I know Kit wants to put something to you. Kit?"

Kit leaned across the table. "I want to play the waiter," he said.

Aurélien thought before answering. "The waiter is only in the film for about two minutes, right at the end."

"Which is why we thought you should meet Naomi."

"The way I see it," Naomi said, "is that Nathalie has been in a relationship with the waiter. That's why she goes to the restaurant. And we could see, in flashback, you know, their relationship."

"I think it could be extraordinary, Aurélien," Lanier said.

"And I know that because of our situation, I and Lanier, our marital situation," Kit added, "we could bring something extraordinary to that relationship. And beautiful."

Lanier and Kit kissed each other, briefly but with some passion, before resuming the argument in favor of the flashback. Aurélien ordered some steak and french fries as they fleshed out the relationship between Nathalie X and her waiter-lover.

"And Naomi would write this?" Aurélien asked.

"Yes," Lanier said. "I'm not ready to work with another writer just yet."

"I think Bob Berger has another writer—Matt Friedrich."

"What's he done?" Kit said.

"We have to let Matt go, Aurélien," Lanier said. "You shouldn't drink beer this early in the morning."

"Why not?"

"I'm an alcoholic," Kit said. "It's the thin edge of the wedge, believe me."

"Could you guys leave me alone with Aurélien?" Lanier said.

They left.

LANIER CROSS. I have a theory about this town: the money doesn't matter. THE MONEY DOESN'T MATTER. Everybody thinks it's about the money but they're wrong. They think it's only because of the money that people put up with the godawful shit that's dumped on them. That there can be only one possible reason why people are prepared to be so desperately unhappy. Money. Not so. Consider this: everybody who matters in this town has more than enough money. They don't need any more money. And I'm not talking about the studio heads, the top directors, the big stars, the people with obscene amounts. There are thousands of people in this town, possibly tens of thousands, who are involved in movies who have more money than is reasonably acceptable. So it's not about money, it can't be, it's about something else. It's about being at the center of the world.

"She loved you," Kaiser Prevost said. "She's all over you like a rash."

"Any news of Delphine?"

"Who? Ah, no. What did you say to her, to Lanier? Bob called, she'll do it for nothing. Well, half her normal fee. Sensational idea about Kit Vermeer. Excellent. Why didn't I think of that? Maybe that's what swung it."

"No, it was her idea. How are we going to finish the film without Delphine?"

"Aurélien. Please. Forget Delphine Drelle. We have Lanier Cross. We fired Friedrich, we got Tashourian writing the flashback. We're in business, my son, in business."

NAOMI TASHOURIAN. I have a theory about this town, this place. Don't be a woman.

Aurélien sat in the cutting room with Barker Lear, an editor, as they ran what existed of *Seeing Through Nathalie* on the Moviola.

Barker, a heavy man with a grizzled ginger goatee, watched Delphine sit down at the pizzeria and order a beer. She drank it down and ordered another, then the sound boom, which had been bobbing erratically in and out of frame for the last few minutes, fell fully into view and the screen went black.

Barker turned and looked at Aurélien, who was frowning and tapping his teeth with the end of a pencil.

"That's some film," Barker said. "Who's the girl, she's extraordinary."

"Delphine Drelle."

"She a big star in France?"

"No."

"Sorta hypnotic effect, she has . . ." He shrugged. "Shame about the boom."

"Oh, I don't worry about that sort of thing," Aurélien said. "It adds to the verisimilitude."

"I don't follow."

"You're meant to know it's a film. That's why the end works so well."

"So what happens in the end? You've still got to shoot it, right?"

"Yes. I don't know what happens. Neither does Delphine."

"You don't say?"

"She gets drunk, you see. We watch her getting drunk. We don't cut away. We don't know what she might do. That's what makes it so exciting—that's 'the destiny of Nathalie X.' "

"I see . . . So, ah, what happened at the end of the first film?"

"She goes to the café, she drinks six or seven beers very quickly, and I can see she's quite drunk. She orders another drink and when the waiter brings it she throws it in his face."

"You don't say? Then what?"

"They have a fight. Delphine and the waiter. They really hit each other. It's fantastic. Delphine, she's had this training, self-defense. She knees this guy in the *couilles*. Boff!"

"Fascinating."

"He falls over. She collapses, crying, she turns to me, swears at me. Runs off into the night. The end. It's amazing."

Barker rubbed his beard, thinking. He glanced at Aurélien covertly.

"Going to do the same thing here?"

"No, no. It's got to be different for the USA, for Hollywood. That's why I gave her the gun."

"Is it a real gun?"

"Oh yes. Otherwise what would be the point?"

BARKER LEAR. I definitely had him for a wacko at first, but after I spent an afternoon with him, talking to him, it seemed to me he really knew what he was doing. He was a real calm guy, Aurélien. He had his own vision, didn't worry about other people, what other people might think of him. And it was the easiest editing job I ever did. Long long takes. Lot of handheld stuff. The walk had a few reverses, a few mid shots, dolly shots. And the film was kind of exciting, I have to admit, and I was really quite disappointed that he still hadn't shot the end. This girl Delphine, with this crazy blond fringe over her eyes, there was definitely something wild about her. I mean, who knows, once she got loaded, what she might have done. Maybe Aurélien wasn't a wacko, but she definitely was.

You know, I have a theory about this town, this place. I've been working here for twenty-five years and I've seen them all. In this town you have very, very clever people and very, very wacko people, and the problem is, and that's what makes this place different, our special problem is the very clever people *have* to work with the very wacko people. They have to, they can't help it, it's the nature of the job. That doesn't happen other places for one simple reason—clever and wacko don't mix.

Aurélien stood by the pool with Nancy enjoying the subdued play of morning light on the water. Today Nancy's hair was white blond and she wore a tutu over her leotard and cowboy boots with spurs. She handed him a pair of car keys and an envelope with a thousand dollars in it.

"That's the new rental car. Celica OK? And there's your per diem. And you've got dinner with Lanier Cross at 6:30."

"6:30 p.m.?"

"Ah, yeah . . . She can make it 6:00 if you prefer. She asked me to tell you it will be vegetarian."

"What are all those men doing? Is it some kind of military exercise?"

"Those are the gardeners. Shall I make them go away?"

"No, it's fine."

"And Tim Pascal called."

"Who's he?"

"He's an English film director. He has several projects in development at Alcazar. He wanted to know if you wanted to lunch or drink or whatever."

The doorbell rang. Aurélien strode across the several levels of his cool white living room to answer it, and as he did so the bell rang twice again. It was Delphine.

KAISER PREVOST. I have a theory about this town; it doesn't represent the fulfillment of the American dream, it represents the fulfillment of an American reality. It rewards relentless persistence, massive stamina, ruthlessness and the ability to live with grotesque failure. Look at me: I am a small-ish guy, 138 pounds, with pretty severe myopia, and near average academic qualifications. But I have a personable manner and an excellent memory and a good head of hair. I will work hard and I will take hard decisions and I have developed the thickest of thick skins. With these attributes in this town nothing can stop me. Or those like me. We are legion. We know what they call us but we don't care. We don't need contacts, we don't need influence, we don't need talent, we don't need cosmetic surgery. That's why I love this place. It allows us to thrive. That's why when I heard Aurélien had never showed for dinner with Lanier Cross, I didn't panic. People like me take that kind of awful crisis in their stride.

Aurélien turned over and gently kissed Delphine's right breast. She stubbed out her cigarette and hunched into him.
   "This house is incredible, Aurélien. I like it here."
   "Where's Holbish?"
   "You promised me you wouldn't mention him again. I'm sorry, Aurélien, I don't know what made me do it."
   "No, I'm just curious."
   "He's gone to Seattle."
   "Well, we can manage without him. Are you ready?"
   "Of course, it's the least I can do. What about the pizzeria?"
   "I was given a thousand dollars' cash today. I knew it would come in useful."

MATT FRIEDRICH. I have to admit I was hoping for the *Seeing Through Nathalie* rewrite. When Bob Berger fired me and said that Naomi Tashourian was the new writer, it hurt for a while. It always does, no matter how successful you are. But in my case I was due a break and I thought Nathalie was it. I've missed out on my last three Guild arbitrations and a Lanier Cross film would have helped, however half-baked, however art-house. Berger said they would honor the fee for the synopsis I did (obfuscation takes on new meaning), but I guess the check is still in the post. But, I do not repine, as a great English novelist once said, I just get on with the job.
   I have a theory about this town, this *Spielraum* where we dream and dawdle: one of our problems—perhaps it's *the* problem—is that here ego always outstrips ability. Always. That applies to everyone: writers, directors, actors, heads of

production, d-boys and unit runners. It's our disease, our mark of Cain. When you have success here you think you can do anything, and that's the great error. The success diet is too rich for our digestive systems: it poisons us, addles the brain. It makes us blind. We lose our self-knowledge. My advice to all those who make it is this: *take the job you would have done if the film had been a flop.* Don't go for the big one, don't let those horizons recede. Do the commercial, the TV pilot, the documentary, the three-week rewrite, the character role or whatever it was you had lined up first. Do that job and then maybe you can reach for the forbidden fruit, but at least you'll have your feet on the ground.

"Kaiser?"

"Bob?"

"He's not at the house, Kaiser."

"Shit."

"He's got to phone her. He's got to apologize."

"No. He's got to lie."

"She called Vincent."

"Fuck. The bitch."

"That's how bad she wants to do it. I think it's a good sign."

"Where is that African bastard? I'll kill him."

"Nancy says the French babe showed."

"Oh, no. No, fuckin' no!"

"It gets worse, Kaiser. Vincent told me to call Tim Pascal."

"Who the fuck's he?"

"Some English director. Lanier wants to meet with him."

"Who's his agent?"

"Sheldon . . . Hello? Kaiser?"

GEORGE MALINVERNO. I got a theory about this town, this place: everybody likes pizza. Even the French. We got to know them real well, I guess. They came back every night, the French. The tall black guy, the ratty one and the blond girl. Real pretty girl. Every night they come. Every night they eat pizza. Every night she ties one on. Everybody likes pizza. [Bitter laugh] Everybody. Too bad I didn't think of it first, huh?

They film one night. And the girl, she's steaming. Then, I don't know, something goes wrong and we don't see them for a while. Then he comes back. Just the black guy, Aurélien and the girl. He says, can they film, one night, a thousand bucks. I say for sure. So he sets up the sound and he sets up the camera behind the bushes. You know it's not a disturbance, exactly. I never see anybody make a film like this before. A thousand bucks, it's very generous. So the girl she walks up, she takes a seat, she orders beer and keeps on drinking. Soon she's pretty stewed. Aurélien sits behind the bushes, just keeps filming. Some guy tries to pick her up, puts his hand on the table, like, leans over, she takes a book of matches, like that one, and does something to the back of his hand with the corner. I couldn't see what she did, but the guy gasps with pain, shudders like this, just backs off.

Then we get a big party in, birthday party, they'd already booked, fourteen people. She sits there drinking and smoking, Aurélien's filming. Then we bring the cake out of the kitchen, candles all lit. Whenever there's a birthday we get Chico to sing. Chico, the little waiter, tubby guy, wanted to be an opera singer. Got a fine strong voice. He's singing "Happy Birthday to You"—he's got a kind of drawn-out, elaborate way of singing it. Top of his voice, *molto vibrato*, you know. Next thing I know the girl's on her feet with a fuckin' gun in her hand, screaming in French. Nobody can hear because Chico's singing his balls off. I tear out from behind the bar, but I'm too late. POW. First shot blows the cake away. BAM. Second one gets Chico in the thigh. Flesh wound, thank God. I charge her to the ground, Roberto jumps on top. We wrestle the gun away. She put up quite a fight for a little thing. Did something to my shoulder too, she twisted it in some way, never been the same since. Aurélien got the whole thing on film. I hear it looks great.

Aurélien sat outside the Alcazar screening room with Kaiser Prevost and Bob Berger. Berger combed and recombed his hair, he kept smelling his comb, smelling his fingertips. He asked Prevost to smell his hair. Prevost said it smelled of shampoo. Prevost went to the lavatory for the fourth time.

"Relax," Aurélien said to them both. "I'm really pleased with the film. I couldn't be more pleased."

Berger groaned. "Don't say that, don't say that."

"If he likes it," Kaiser said, "we're in business. Lanier will like it, for sure, and Aurélien will apologize. Won't you, Aurélien? Of course you will. No problem. Lanier loved him. Lanier loved you, didn't she, Aurélien?"

"Why are we worried about Lanier?" Aurélien said. "Delphine came back. We finished the film."

"Jesus Christ," said Bob Berger.

"Don't worry, Bob," Kaiser said. "Everything can be fixed."

Vincent Bandine emerged from the screening room.

Aurélien stood up. "What do you think?"

VINCENT BANDINE. I believe in candor. I have a theory about this town, this place: we don't put enough stock in candor. I am into candor in a big way. So I take Aurélien aside, gently, and I say, "Aurélien, or whatever your name is, I think your film is goatshit. I think it's a disgusting boring piece of Grade A manure. I wouldn't give the sweat off my balls for your goatshit film." That's what I said, verbatim. And I have to give it to the kid, he just stood there and looked at me, sort of a slight smile on his face. Usually when I'm this candid they're in deep shock, or weeping, or vomiting by now. And he looks at me and says, "I can't blame you for thinking like this. You're not a man of culture, so I can't blame you for thinking like this." And he walks. He walks out jauntily. I should have had his fucking legs broken. I've got the biggest collection of Vuillard paintings on the West Coast of America. I should have had his fucking legs broken. We had to pay the waiter fifty grand not to press charges, keep the Alcazar name out of things. The girl went to a clinic for three weeks to dry out . . . Aurélien No. Not a man of culture, eh?

KIT VERMEER. Ah, Lanier took it badly. I don't think that. Do you mind? Thank you. Bats and lemurs, man, wow, they didn't get a look in. Bats and lemurs. Story of my life. *Weltanschauung*, that's what I'm up for. No, *Weltschmerz*. That's my bag. Bats and lemurs. Why not owls and armadillos? No, I'm not looking at you, sir, or talking to you. Forsooth. Fuckin' nerd. Wank in a bath, that's what an English friend of mine calls them. What a wank in a bath. Owls and armadillos.

MATT FRIEDRICH. Aurélien came to see me before he left, which was gracious of him, I thought, especially for a film director, and he told me what had happened. I commiserated and told him other sorry stories about this town, this place. But he needed no consoling. "I enjoyed my visit," he said. "No, I did. And I made the film. It was a curious but interesting experience."

"It's just a dance," I think I remember saying to him. "It's just a dance we have to do."

He laughed. He found that funny.

END ROLLER

BOB BERGER
is working from home,
where he is writing several screenplays

DELPHINE DRELLE
plays the character "Suzi de la Tour" in
NBC's *Till Darkness Falls*

KAISER PREVOST
works for the investment bank Harbinger Cohen
in New York City

MARIUS NO
is in his first year at l'Ecole Supérieure
des Etudes Cinématographiques

BERTRAND HOLBISH
manages the Seattle band "Morbid Anatomy"

NAOMI TASHOURIAN
has written her first novel, *Credits Not Contractual*

MICHAEL SCOTT GEHN
is chief executive critic and on the
editorial board of *film/e*

KIT VERMEER
is a practicing Sikh and wishes to be known as
Khalsa Hari Atmar

LANIER CROSS
is scheduled to star in Lucy Wang's film
Charles Baudelaire's Les Fleurs du Mal

GEORGE MALINVERNO
has opened a third pizzeria in Pacific Palisades

VINCENT BANDINE
has announced Alcazar Films' eighteen-picture slate
for the coming year

BARKER LEAR
lives in San Luis Obispo

MATT FRIEDRICH
has taken his own life

"NATHALIE X AUX ETATS-UNIS"
has been nominated for an Academy Award
in the "Best Foreign Film" category

AURÉLIEN NO
is not returning your calls

Transfigured Night

From my tenth or eleventh year I remember the following incident:

> box on the ear
> looking for a gymnasium   Aryan origin
> Gymnasium   love for Erich
>   fight
> relation to Paul
>   to Gretl
>   to Rudi   good memories

Wolfrum   I attempt to win him over and entice him away from my brother

>   being in love   Paul a mischief-maker
>   innocent expression
>   lewdness

Latin exercises for Papa   thoughts of suicide

The private papers of Ludwig Wittgenstein

SELBSTMORD

In this city, and at this time, you should understand that suicide was a completely acceptable option, an entirely understandable, rational course of action to take. And I speak as one who knows its temptations intimately: three of my elder brothers took their own lives—Hans, Rudi and Kurt. That left Paul, me

37

and my three older sisters. My sisters, I am sure, were immune to suicide's powerful contagion. I cannot speak for Paul. As for myself, I can only say that its clean resolution of all my problems—intellectual and emotional—was always most appealing; that open door to oblivion always beckoned to me and, odd though it may seem, suicide—the idea of suicide—lies at the very foundation of all my work in ethics and logic.

THE BENEFACTOR

I came down from the Hochreith, our house in the country, to Vienna especially to meet Herr Ficker. The big white villa in the parks of Neuwaldegg was closed up for the summer. I had one of the gardeners prepare my room and make up a bed, and his wife laid the table on the terrace and helped me cook dinner. We were to have *Naturschnitzel* with *Kochsalat* with a cold bottle of Zöbinger. Simple, honest food. I hoped Ficker would notice.

I shaved and dressed and went out onto the terrace to wait for him to arrive. I was wearing a lemon-yellow, soft-collared shirt with no tie and a light tweed jacket that I had bought years before in Manchester. Its fraying cuffs had been repaired, in the English way, with a dun green leather. My hair was clean and still damp, my face was cool, scraped smooth. I drank a class of sherbet water as I waited for Ficker. The evening light was milky and diffused, as if hung with dust. I could hear the faint noise of motors and carriages on the roads of Neuwaldegg and in the gathering dusk I could make out the figure of the gardener moving about in the allée of pleached limes. A fleeting but palpable peace descended on me and I thought for some minutes of David and our holidays together in Iceland and Norway. I missed him.

Ficker was an earnest young man, taller than me (mind you, I am not particularly tall) with fine thinning hair brushed back off his brow. He wore spectacles with crooked wire frames, as if he had accidentally sat upon them and had hastily straightened them out himself. He was neatly and soberly dressed, wore no hat and was clean-shaven. His lopsided spectacles suggested a spirit of frivolity and facetiousness that, I soon found out, was entirely inaccurate.

I had already explained to him, by letter, about my father's death, my legacy and how I wished to dispose of a proportion of it. He had agreed to my conditions and promised to respect my demand for total anonymity. We talked, in businesslike fashion, about the details but I could sense, as he expressed his gratitude, strong currents of astonishment and curiosity.

Eventually he had to ask, "But why me? Why my magazine . . . in particular?"

I shrugged. "It seemed to be exemplary, of its sort. I like its attitude, its, its seriousness. And besides, your writers seem the most needy."

"Yes . . . That's true." He was none the wiser.

"It's a family trait. My father was a great benefactor—to musicians mainly. We just like to do it."

Ficker then produced a list of writers and painters he thought were the most deserving. I glanced through it: very few of the names were familiar to me, and beside each one Ficker had written an appropriate sum of money. Two names, at the top of the list, were to receive by far the largest amounts.

"I know of Rilke, of course," I said, "and I'm delighted you chose him. But who's he?" I pointed to the other. "Why should he get so much? What does he do?"

"He's a poet," Ficker said. "I think . . . well, no man on this list will benefit more from your generosity. To be completely frank, I think it might just save his life."

SCHUBERT

My brother Hans drowned himself in Chesapeake Bay. He was a musical prodigy who gave his first concert in Vienna at the age of nine. I never really knew him. My surviving brother Paul was also musically gifted, a brilliant pianist who was a pupil of Leschetizky and made his debut in 1913. I remember Paul saying to me once that of all musical tastes the love of Schubert required the least explanation. When one thinks of the huge misery of his life and sees in his work no trace of it at all—sees the complete absence in his music of all bitterness.

THE BANK

I had arranged with Ficker that I would be in the Öster-reichische Nationalbank on Swarzspanierstrasse at three o'clock. I was there early and sat down at a writing desk in a far corner. It was quiet and peaceful: the afternoon rush had yet to begin and the occasional sound of heels on the marble floor as clients crossed from the entrance foyer to the rows of counters was soothing, like the background click of ivory dominoes or the ceramic kiss of billiard balls in the gaming room of my favorite café near the art schools . . .

Ficker was on time and accompanied by our poet. Ficker caught my eye and I gave a slight nod and then bent my head over the spectral papers on my desk. Ficker went to a teller's guichet to inquire about the banker's draft, leaving the poet standing momentarily alone in the middle of the marble floor, gazing around him like a peasant at the high dim vaults of the ceiling and the play of afternoon sunshine on the ornamental brasswork of the chandeliers.

Georg———, as I shall refer to him, was a young man, twenty-seven years old—two years older than me—small and quite sturdily built, and, like many small men, seemed to have been provided with a head designed for a bigger body alto-gether. His head was crude- and heavy-looking, its propor-tions exaggerated by his bristly, close-cropped hair. He was clean-shaven. He had a weak mouth, the upper lip overhung the bottom one slightly, and a thick triangular nose. He had low brows and slightly Oriental-looking, almond-shaped eyes. He was what my mother would have called "an ugly customer."

He stood now, looking expressionlessly about him, swaying slightly, as if buffeted by an invisible crowd. He appeared at once ill and strong—pale-faced, ugly, dark-eyed, but with something about the set of his shoulders, the way his feet were planted on the ground, that suggested reserves of strength. Indeed, the year before, Ficker had told me, he had almost died from an overdose of Veronal that would have killed an ordinary man in an hour or two. Since his school days, it transpired, he had been a compulsive user of narcotic drugs and was also an immoderate drinker. At school he used chloroform to intoxicate himself. He was now a qualified dispensing chemist, a career he had taken up, so Ficker informed me, solely because it gave him access to more effective drugs. I found this single-mindedness oddly impressive. To train for two years at the University of Vienna as a pharmacist, to pass the necessary exams to qualify, testified to an uncommon dedication. Ficker had given me some of his poems to read. I could not understand them at all; their images for me were strangely haunting and evocative but finally entirely opaque. But I liked their *tone;* their tone seemed to me to be quite remarkable.

I watched him now, discreetly, as Ficker completed the preliminary documentation and signaled him over to endorse the banker's draft. Ficker—I think this was a mistake—presented the check to him with a small flourish and shook him by the hand, as if he had just won first prize in a lottery. I could sense that Georg knew very little of what was going on. I saw him turn the check over immediately so as to hide the amount from his own eyes. He exchanged a few urgent words with Ficker, who smiled encouragingly and patted him on the arm. Ficker was very happy, almost gleeful—in his role as the philanthropist's go-between he was vicariously enjoying what he imagined would be Georg's astonishment. But he was wrong. I knew it the instant Georg turned over the check and read the amount: 20,000 crowns. A thriving dispensing chemist would have to work six or seven years to earn a similar sum. I saw the check flutter and tremble in his fingers. I saw Georg blanch and swallow violently several times. He put the back of his hand to his lips and his shoulders heaved. He reached out to a pillar for support, bending over from the waist. His body convulsed in a spasm as he tried to control his writhing stomach. I knew then that he was an honest man for he had the honest man's profound fear of extreme good fortune. Ficker snatched the check from his shaking fingers as Georg appeared to totter. He uttered a faint cry as warm bile and vomit shot from his mouth to splash and splatter on the cool marble of the Nationalbank's flagged floor.

A GOOD LIFE — A GOOD DEATH

I got to know Ficker quite well over our various meetings about the division and disposal of my benefaction. Once in our discussions the subject of suicide came up and he seemed genuinely surprised when I told him that scarcely a day went by when I did not think about it. But I explained to him that if I could not get along with life and the world, then to commit suicide would be the ultimate admission of failure. I pointed out that this notion was the very essence of ethics and morality. For if anything is not to be allowed, then surely that must be suicide. For if suicide is allowed, then anything is allowed.

Sometimes I think that a good life should end in a death that one could welcome. Perhaps, even, it is only a good death that allows us to call a life "good."

Georg, I believe, has nearly died many times. For example, shortly before the Veronal incident he almost eliminated himself by accident. Georg lived for a time in Innsbruck. One night, after a drinking bout in a small village near the city, he decided to walk home. At some stage on his journey back, overcome by tiredness, he decided to lie down in the snow and sleep. When he awoke in the morning the world had been replaced by a turbid white void. For a moment he thought . . . but almost immediately he realized he had been covered in the night by a new fall of snow. In fact it was about forty centimeters deep. He heaved himself to his feet, brushed off his clothes and, with a clanging, gonging headache, completed his journey to Innsbruck. Ficker related all this to me.

How I wish I had been passing that morning! The first sleepy traveler along that road when Georg awoke. In the still, crepuscular light, that large lump on the verge begins to stir, some cracks and declivities suddenly deform the smooth contours, then a fist punches free and finally that crude ugly face emerges, with its frosty beret of snow, staring stupidly, blinking, spitting . . .

THE WAR

The war saved my life. I really do not know what I would have done without it. On 7 August, the day war was declared on Russia, I enlisted as a volunteer gunner in the artillery for the duration and was instructed to report to a garrison artillery regiment in Cracow. In my elation I was reluctant to go straight home to pack my bags (my family had by now all returned to Vienna), so I took a taxi to the Café Museum.

I should say that I joined the army because it was my civic duty, yet I was even more glad to enlist because I knew at that time I had to *do* something, I had to subject myself to the rigors of a harsh routine that would divert me from my intellectual work. I had reached an impasse and the impossibility of ever proceeding further filled me with morbid despair.

By the time I reached the Café Museum it was about six o'clock in the evening. (I liked this café because its interior was modern: its square rooms were lined with square honey-

colored oak paneling, hung with prints of drawings by
Charles Dana Gibson.) Inside, it was busy, the air noisy with
speculation about the war. It was warm and muggy, the atmosphere suffused with the reek of beer and cigar smoke. The
patrons were mostly young men, students from the nearby art
schools, clean-shaven, casually and unaffectedly dressed. So I
was a little surprised to catch a glimpse in one corner of a uniform. I pushed through the crowd to see who it was.

Georg, it was obvious, was already fairly drunk. He sat
strangely hunched over, staring intently at the tabletop. His
posture and the ferocious concentration of his gaze clearly put
people off, as the three other seats around his table remained
unoccupied. I told a waiter to bring a half-liter of Heuniger
Wein to the table and then sat down opposite him.

Georg was wearing the uniform of an officer, a lieutenant,
in the Medical Corps. He looked at me candidly and without
resentment, and, of course, without any sign of recognition.
He seemed much the same as the last time I had seen him, at
once ill-looking and possessed of a sinewy energy. I introduced myself and told him I was pleased to see a fellow soldier
as I myself had just enlisted.

"It's your civic duty," he said, his voice strong and un-
slurred. "Have a cigar."

He offered me a trabuco, those ones that have a straw
mouthpiece because they are so strong. I declined—at that
time I did not smoke. When the wine arrived he insisted on
paying for it.

"I'm a rich man," he said as he filled our glasses. "Where're
you posted?"

"Galicia."

"Ah, the Russians are coming." He paused. "I want to go
somewhere cold and dark. I detest this sun, and this city. Why
aren't we fighting the Eskimos? I hate daylight. Maybe I could
declare war on the Lapps. One-man army."

"Bit lonely, no?"

"I want to be lonely. All I do is pollute my mind talking to people . . . I want a dark cold lonely war. Please."

"People will think you're mad."

He raised his glass. "God preserve me from sanity."

I thought of something Nietzsche had said: "Our life, our happiness, is beyond the north, beyond ice, beyond death." I looked into Georg's ugly face, his thin eyes and glossy lips, and felt a kind of love for him and his honesty. I clinked my glass against his and asked God to preserve me from sanity as well.

Tagebuch: 15 August. Cracow.

. . . If your wife, for example, continually puts too much sugar in your tea it is not because she has too much sugar in her cupboard, it is because she is not educated in the ways of handling sweetness. Similarly, the problem of how to live a good life cannot ever be solved by continually assaulting it with the intellect. Certain things can only be shown, not stated . . .

THE SEARCHLIGHT

I enlisted in the artillery to fire howitzers but instead found myself manning a searchlight on a small, heavily armed paddle steamer called the *Goplana*. We cruised up and down the Vistula, ostensibly looking for Russians but also to provide support for any river crossings by our own forces.

I enjoyed my role in charge of the searchlight. I took its mounting apart and oiled and greased its bearings. Reassembled, it moved effortlessly under the touch of my fingers. Its strong beam shone straight and true in the blurry semidarkness of those late summer nights. However, I soon found the living conditions on the *Goplana* intolerable because of the stink, the proximity and the vulgarity of my fellow soldiers. And because we were constantly in motion, life belowdecks was dominated by the thrum and grind of the *Goplana*'s churning paddles. I spent long hours in my corner of the bridge house needlessly overhauling the mechanism of the searchlight—anything to escape the torrent of filth and viciousness that poured from the men. But despite these periods of solitude and isolation I found that my old despair began to creep through me again, like a stain.

One day we disembarked at Sandomierz and were sent to a bathhouse. As we washed I looked at my naked companions, their brown faces and forearms, their gray-white bodies and dark, dripping genitals as they soaped and sluiced themselves with garrulous ostentation. I felt only loathing for them, my fellow men. It was impossible both to work with them and to have nothing to do with them. I was glad that I felt no stirrings of sensuality as I contemplated their naked bodies. I saw that they were men but I could not see they were human beings.

Tagebuch: 8 September. Sawichost.

. . . The news is worse. All the talk is of Cracow being besieged. Last night there was an alarm. I ran up on deck to man the searchlight. It was raining and I wore only a shirt and trousers. I played the beam of the searchlight to and fro on the opposite bank of the river for hours, my feet and hands slowly becoming numb. Then we heard the sound of gunfire and I at once became convinced I was going to die that night. The beam of the searchlight was a lucent arrow pointing directly at me. And for the first time I felt, being face-to-face with my own death, with possibly only an hour or two of life remaining to me, that I had in those few hours the chance to be a good man, if only because of this uniquely potent consciousness of myself. And, as ever, my attempts to articulate my experience as I understood and *felt* it, and to seize intellectually its profound implications, slipped beyond the power of language. "I did my duty and stayed at my post." That is all I can say about that tremendous night.

THE AMPUTEE

Of course I did not die and of course I fell back into more abject moods of self-disgust and loathing. Perhaps the only consolation was that my enormous fatigue made it impossible for me to think about my work.

It was about this time—in September or October—that I heard the news about my brother Paul. He was a quite different personality from me—fierce and somewhat dominating—and he had tackled his vocation as concert pianist with uncompromising dedication. Since his debut his future seemed assured, an avenue of bright tomorrows. To receive the news, then, that he had been captured by the Russians and had had his right arm amputated at the elbow, as the result of wounds he had sustained, was devastating. For days my thoughts were of Paul and of what I would do in his situation. Poor Paul, I thought, if only there were some solution other than suicide. What philosophy it will take to get over this!

Tagebuch: 13 October. Nadbrzesze.

. . . We have sailed here, waited for twelve hours and have now been ordered to return to Sawichost. All day we can hear the mumble of artillery in the east. I find myself drawn down into dark depression again, remorselessly. Why? What is the real basis of this malaise? . . . I see one of my fellow soldiers pissing over the side of the boat in full view of the few citizens of Nadbrzesze who have gathered on the quayside to stare at us. The long pale arc of his urine sparkles in the thin autumn sunshine. Another soldier leans on his elbows staring candidly at the man's flaccid white penis, held daintily between two fingers like a titbit. This is shaken, its tip squeezed and then tucked away in the coarse serge of his trousers. I think if I were standing at a machine gun rather than at a searchlight I could kill them both without a qualm . . . Why do I detest these simple foolish men so? Why can I not be impassive? I despise my own weakness, my inability to distance myself from the commonplace.

THE BATTLE OF GRÓDEK

On our return from Sawichost I received mail. A long letter from David—I wonder if he thinks of me half as much as I think of him?—and a most distressing communication from Ficker, to whom I had written asking for some books to be sent to me. I quote:

> . . . I see from your letter that you are not far from Cracow. I wonder if you get the opportunity you could attempt to find and visit [Georg]. You may have heard of the heavy fighting at Gródek some two weeks ago. Georg was there and, owing to the chaos and disorganization that prevailed at the time, was mistakenly placed in charge of a field hospital not far behind our lines. Apparently he protested vigorously that he was merely a dispensing chemist and not a doctor, but resources were so stretched he was told to do the best he could.
>
> Thus Georg found himself with two orderlies (Czechs, who spoke little German) in charge of a fifty-bed field hospital. As the battle wore on more than ninety severely wounded casualties were delivered during the day. Repeatedly, Georg signaled for a doctor to be sent as he could do nothing for these men except inject them with morphine and attempt to dress their wounds. In fact it became clear that through some oversight these casualties had been sent to the wrong hospital. The ambulance crews that transported them had been erroneously informed that there was a field surgery and a team of surgeons operating there.

By nine in the evening all of Georg's supplies of morphine were exhausted. Shortly thereafter men began to scream from the resurgent pain. Finally, one officer who had lost his left leg at the hip shot himself in the head.

At this point Georg ran away. Two kilometers from the field hospital was a small wood that, at the start of the battle, had been a battalion headquarters. Georg went there for help, or at least to report the ghastly condition of the wounded in his charge. When he arrived there he found that an impromptu military tribunal had just executed twenty deserters by hanging.

I do not know exactly what happened next. I believe that at the sight of these fresh corpses Georg tried to seize a revolver from an officer and shoot himself. Whatever happened, he behaved in a demented manner, was subdued and himself arrested for desertion in the face of the enemy. I managed to visit him briefly in the mental hospital at Cracow ten days ago. He is in a very bad way, but at least, thank God, the charges of desertion have been dropped and he is being treated for dementia praecox. For some reason Georg is convinced he will be prosecuted for cowardice. He is sure he is going to hang.

THE ASYLUM AT CRACOW

Georg's cell was very cold, and dark, the only illumination coming from an oil lamp in the corridor. Georg needed a shave but otherwise he looked much the same as he had on my two previous encounters with him. He was wearing a curious oatmeal canvas uniform, the jacket secured with strings instead of buttons. With his big head and thin eyes he looked strangely Chinese. There was one other patient in his cell with him, a major in the cavalry who was suffering from delirium tremens. This man remained hunched on a truckle bed in the corner of the room, sobbing quietly to himself while Georg and I spoke. He did not recognize me. I merely introduced myself as a friend of Ficker's.

"Ficker asked me to visit you," I said. "How are you?"

"Well, I'm . . ." He stopped and gestured at the major. "I used to think I was a heavy drinker." He smiled. "Actually, he's being quite good now." Georg rubbed his short hair with both hands.

"I heard about what happened," I said. "It must have been terrible."

He looked at me intently, and then seemed to think for a while.

"Yes," he said, "yes, yes, yes. All that sort of thing."

"I completely understand."

He shrugged uselessly. Certain things can only be shown, not stated.

He smiled. "You don't have any cigars on you, by any chance? They haven't brought me my kit. One longs for a decent cigar."

"Let me get some for you."

"I smoke trabucos—the ones with the straw holder."

"They're very strong, I believe. I don't smoke, but I heard they can burn your throat."

"It's a small price to pay."

We sat in silence for a moment, listening to the major's snufflings.

"It's very cold here," Georg began slowly, "and very dark, and if they got rid of the major the conditions would be perfect."

"I know what you mean."

"Actually, I have several boxes of trabucos in my kit," he went on. "If you could get a message to my orderly, perhaps he could bring me a couple."

"Of course."

"Oh, and would you ask him to bring me my green leather case."

"Green leather case."

"Yes," he paused. "That is essential . . ." He rubbed his

face, as if his features were tired of being eternally composed. "I think with a good cigar I could even tolerate the major."

I found Georg's orderly in the Medical Corps' billet in a small village on the outskirts of Cracow. The city was clearly visible across the flat cropped meadows where a few piebald ponies grazed: a low attenuated silhouette punctuated by a few domes and spires and the odd factory chimney. In the indistinct grainy light of the late afternoon the bulk of the Marienkirche had the look of a vast warehouse. I passed on Georg's instructions: two boxes of trabuco cigars and his green leather case.

"How is the lieutenant?" the orderly asked.

"He's very well," I said. "Considering . . . Very well indeed."

Georg died that night from a heart seizure brought on by a massive intravenous injection of cocaine. According to his orderly, who was the last person to speak to him, he was "in a state of acute distress" and must have misjudged the dose.

Tagebuch: 10 November. Sawichost.

. . . The simplest way to describe the book of moral philosophy that I am writing is that it concerns what can and cannot be said. In fact it will be only half a book. The most interesting half will be the one that I cannot write. That half will be the most eloquent.

TEA AT NEUWALDEGG

It is springtime. After a shower of rain we take tea on the terrace of the big house at Neuwaldegg. Me, my mother, my sisters Helen and Hermine—and Paul. I am on leave; Paul has just been returned from captivity as part of an exchange of wounded prisoners. He sits with his right sleeve neatly pinned up, awkwardly squeezing lemon into his tea with his left hand. I think of Georg and I look at Paul. His hair is graying, his clothes are immaculate.

Quite suddenly he announces that he is going to continue with his career as a concert pianist and teach himself to play with the left hand only. He proposes to commission pieces for the left hand from Richard Strauss and Ravel. There is silence, and then I say, "Bravo, Paul. Bravo." And, spontaneously, we all clap for him.

The modest sound of our applause carries out over the huge garden. A faint breeze shifts the new spring foliage of the chestnut trees, glistening after the rain, and the gardener, who has just planted a bed of geraniums, looks up from his work for a moment, smiles bemusedly at us, clambers to his feet and bows.

Hôtel des Voyageurs

Hôtel de la Louisiane.

Me for good talk, wet evenings, intimacy, *vins rouges en carafe*, reading, relative solitude, street worship . . . shop gazing, alley sloping, café crawling . . . I am for the intricacy of Europe, the discreet and many-folded strata of the Old World, the past, the North, the world of ideas. I am for the Hôtel de la Louisiane.

CYRIL CONNOLLY,
Journal, 1928–1937

Thursday, 26 July 1928

PARIS. Boat train from London strangely quiet. I had a whole compartment to myself. Fine drizzle at the Gare du Nord. After breakfast I spent two hours trying to telephone Louise in London. I finally got through and a man's voice answered. "Who's calling?" he said, very abruptly. "Tell Louise it's Logan Mountstewart," I said, equally brusquely. Longish silence. Then the man said Louise was in Hampshire. I kept telling him that Louise was never in Hampshire during the week. Eventually I realized it was Robbie. He refused to admit it so I called him every foul name I could think of and hung up.

Lonely bitter evening, drank too much. A protracted street prowl through the Marais. The thought of Louise with Robbie made me want to vomit. Robbie: *faux bonhomme* and fascist shit.

Friday

More rain. I cabled Douglas and Sylvia in Bayonne and told them I was driving down. I then hired the biggest car I could find in Paris, a vast American thing called a Packard, a great beast of a vehicle, with huge bulbous headlamps. I set off after lunch in a thunderstorm, resolved to drive through the night. The south, the south, at last. That's where I will find my peace. Intense disgust at the banality of my English life. How I detest London and all my friends. Except Sholto, perhaps. And Hermione. And Sophie.

Saturday

Crossed the Loire and everything changed. Blue skies, a mineral flinty sun hammering down. *Beau ciel, vrai ciel, regarde moi qui change.* Opened every window in the Packard and drove in a warm buffeting breeze.

Lunch in Angoulême. Ham and Moselle. I had a sudden urge to take Douglas and Sylvia some sweet Monbazillac as a present. Drove on to Libourne and then up the river to Saint-Foy. I turned off the main road, trying to remember the little château we had visited before, in '26, near a place called Pomport.

I must have missed a sign because I found myself in a part of the countryside I did not recognize, in a narrow valley with dark woods at its rim. Blond wind-combed wheat fields stirred silently on either side, the road no longer metaled. And that was when the clanking started in the Packard's engine.

I stopped and raised the bonnet. A hot oily smell, a wisp of something. Smoke? Steam? I stood there in the gathered, broiling heat of the afternoon wondering what to do.

A goatish farmer in a pony and trap understood my request for a "garage" and directed me up a dusty lane.

There was a village, he said, Saint-Barthélemy.

Saint-Barthélemy: one street of ancient shuttered houses, with pocked honey-colored walls. A church with a hideous new spire, quite out of proportion. I found the garage by a bridge over the torpid stream that wound around the village. The *garagiste*, a genial young man in horn-rimmed spectacles, looked at the Packard in frank amazement and said he would have to send to Bergerac for the part he needed. How long would that take, I asked. He shrugged. A day, two days, who knows? And besides, he said, pointing to a glossy limousine up on blocks, he had to finish Monsieur le Comte's car first. There was a hotel I could stay in, he said, at the other end of the village. The Hôtel des Voyageurs.

Sunday

Dinner in the hotel last night. Stringy roast chicken and a rough red wine. I was alone in the dining room, served by an ancient wheezing man, when the hotel's other guest arrived. A woman. She was tall and slim, her dark brown hair cut in a fashionable bob. She wore a dress of cobalt blue crêpe de chine, with a short skirt gathered at the hips. She barely glanced at me and treated the old waiter with brutal abruptness. She was French, or else completely bilingual, and everything about her was redolent of wealth and prestige. At first glance her face seemed not pretty, a little hard, with a slightly hooked nose, but as I covertly gazed at her across the dining room, studying her features as she picked at her meal, her face's shadowed planes and angles, the slight pout of the upper lip, the perfect plucked arcs of her eyebrows, began to assume a fascinating worldly beauty. She ordered a coffee and smoked a cigarette, never once looking in my direction. I was about to invite her to join me for a *digestif* when she stood up and left the room. As she passed the table she looked at me for the first time, squarely, with a casual candid curiosity.

Slept well. For the first time since leaving London did not dream of Louise.

Monday

Encountered the woman in the hotel's small garden. I was sitting at a tin table beneath a chestnut tree, spreading fig jam on a croissant, when I heard her call.

"Thierry?"

I turned, and her face fell. She apologized for interrupting me, she said she thought I was someone else, the linen jacket I was wearing had made her think I was her husband. He had one very similar, the same hair color too. I introduced myself. She said she was la Comtesse de Benoît-Voulon.

"Your husband is staying here?" I asked. She was tall, her eyes were almost on the same level as mine. I could not help noticing the way the taupe silk singlet she wore clung to her breasts. Her eyes were very pale brown, they seemed to look at me with unusual curiosity.

She told me her husband was visiting his mother. The arc of an eyebrow lifted. "The old lady and I . . ." She paused diplomatically. "We do not enjoy each other's company so, so I prefer to wait in the hotel. And besides, our car is being repaired."

"So is mine," I said with a silly laugh, which I instantly regretted. "Quite a coincidence."

"Yes," she said thoughtfully, frowning. That curious glance again. "It is, isn't it?"

To fill my empty day I walked to the next village, called Argenson, and lunched on a tough steak and a delicious tangy *vin rouge en carafe*. On the way back I was given a lift in a lorry piled high with sappy pine logs. My nose prickled with resin all the way back to Saint-Barthélemy.

The hotel was quiet, no one was in the lobby. My key was missing from its hook behind the desk so I assumed the maid was still cleaning the room. Upstairs, the door was very slightly ajar, the room beyond dark and shuttered against the sun. I stepped inside. La Comtesse de Benoît-Voulon was lifting a book from my open suitcase.

"Mr. Mountstewart," she said, the guilt and surprise absent from her face within a second. "I'm so glad you decided to come back early."

Monday

I must make sure I have this right. Must make sure I forget nothing.

We made love in the cool afternoon darkness of my room. There was a strange relaxed confidence about it all, as if it had been prefigured in some way, in the unhurried, tolerant manner our bodies moved to accommodate each other. And afterward we chatted, like old friends. Her name, she said, was Giselle. They were going to Hyères, they had a house there. They always spent August in Hyères, she and her husband.

Then she turned to face me and said: "Logan? . . . Have we ever met before?"

I laughed. "I think I would have remembered."

"Perhaps you know Thierry? Perhaps I've seen you with Thierry."

"Definitely not."

She cradled my face in her hands and stared fiercely at me. She said in a quiet voice, "He didn't send you, did he? If he did you must tell me now." Then she herself laughed, when she saw my baffled look, heard my baffled protestations. "Forget it," she said. "I always think he's playing tricks on me. He's like that, Thierry, with his games."

I slept that afternoon, and when I awoke she had gone. Downstairs, the old waiter had set only one table for dinner. I asked where the lady was and he said she had paid her bill and left the hotel.

At the garage the limousine had gone. The young *garagiste* proudly brandished the spare part for my Packard and said it would be ready tomorrow. I pointed at the empty blocks where the count's car had been.

"Did he come for his car?"

"Two hours ago."

"With his wife?"

"Who?"

"Was there a woman with him, a lady?"

"Oh yes." The *garagiste* smiled at me and offered me one of his yellow cigarettes, which I accepted. "Every year he spends two days with his mother, on his way south. Every year there's a different one."

"Different wife?"

He looked at me knowingly. He drew heavily on his cigarette, his eyes wistfully distant. "They're from Paris, these girls. Amazing." He shook his head in frustrated admiration. Once a year Saint-Barthélemy was graced by one of these astonishing women, he said, these radiant visitors. They stayed in the Hôtel des Voyageurs . . . One day, one day he was going to go to Paris and see them for himself.

Tuesday

At the Café Riche et des Sports in Bergerac, I finish my article on Sainte-Beuve. I pour a cognac into my coffee and compose a telegram to Douglas canceling my visit. *O qu'ils sont pittoresques les trains manqués!* That will not be my fate. I unfold my road map and plot a route to Hyères.

Never Saw Brazil

O N O N E of the sunniest of bright May mornings Senator Dom Liceu Maximiliano Lobo needlessly ran
his comb through his neat goatee and ordered his
chauffeur to pull off to the side of the road. On mornings like
these he liked to walk the remaining five hundred meters to
his office, which he maintained, out of sentiment's sake, and
because of the sea breezes, in Salvador's Cidada Alta. He
sauntered along the sidewalks, debating pleasantly whether to
linger a moment with a coffee and a newspaper on the terrace
of the hotel, or whether to stop off at Olímpia's little apartment, which he kept for her, at very reasonable expense, in
an old colonial building in a square near the cathedral. She
would not be expecting him, and it might be an amusing, not
to say sensuous, experience to dally an hour or so this early
before the day's work called. How bright the sun was, this fine
morning, Senator Dom Liceu Maximiliano Lobo thought as
he turned toward the cathedral, his heels ringing on the cob-
bles, and how vivid the solar benefaction made the geraniums.
Life was indeed good.

The name was the problem, he saw. The problem lay there, definitely. Because . . . Because if you were not happy with your name, he realized, then a small but sustained lifelong stress was imposed on your psyche, your sense of self. It was like being condemned to wear too small shoes all the time; you could still get about but there would always be a pinching, a corn or two aching, something unnaturally hobbled about your gait.

Wesley Bright. Wesley. Bright.

The trouble with his name was that it wasn't *quite* stupid enough—he was not a Wesley Bilderbeest or a Wesley Bugger; in fact it was *almost* a good name. If he had been Wesley Blade, say, or Wesley Beauregard he would have no complaints.

"Wesley?"

Janice passed him the docket. He clicked the switch on the mike.

"Four-seven? Four-seven?"

Silence. Just the permanent death rattle of the ether.

Four-seven answered. "Four-seven."

"Parcel, four-seven. Pick up at Track-Track. Going to Heathrow, as directed."

"Account?"

Wesley sighed. "Yes, four-seven. We do not do cash."

"Oh yeah. Roger, Rog."

He could always change his name, he supposed. Roger, perhaps. Roger Bright. Wesley Roger . . . No. There was that option, though: choose a new moniker, a new handle. But he wondered about that too: hard to shake off an old name, he would guess. It was the way you thought of yourself, after all, your tag on the pigeonhole. And when you were young, you never thought your name was odd—it was a source of dissatisfaction that came with aging, a realization that one didn't really like being a "Wesley Bright" sort of person at all. In his case it had started at college, this chafing, this discomfort. He wondered about these fellows, actors and rock musicians, who called themselves Tsar, or Zane Zorro or DJ Sofaman . . . He was sure that, to themselves, they were always Norman Sidcup or Wilbur Dongdorfer in their private moments.

Colonel Liceu "o Falção" Lobo opened his eyes and he saw that the sun had risen sharp and green through the leafmass outside his bedroom. He shifted and stretched and felt the warm flank of Nilda brush his thigh. He eased himself out of bed and stood naked in the greenbright gloom. He freed his sweaty balls, tugging delicately at his scrotum. He rubbed his face and chest, inhaled, walked quietly out onto the balcony and felt the cool morning on his nakedness. He stood there, the wooden planks rough beneath his bare feet, and leaned on the balustrade looking at the beaten-earth parade ground his battalion had spent two weeks clearing out of the virgin jungle. There was nothing like a new parade ground, Colonel Liceu Lobo thought, with a thin smile of satisfaction, to signal you were here to stay.

He saw Sergeant Elias Galvão emerge from the latrines and amble across the square toward the battalion mess, tightening his belt as he went. A good man, Galvão, a professional, up this early too. "Morning, Sergeant," Colonel Licen Lobo called from his balcony. Sergeant Elias Galvão came abruptly to attention, swiveled to face his naked colonel and saluted.

"Carry on," Colonel Liceu Lobo instructed. Not a flicker on his impassive face, excellent. Sergeant Galvão's lieutenant's pips could not be long away.

"Liceu?" Nilda's husky sleepy voice came from the bedroom. "Where are you?" The colonel felt his manhood stir, as

if of its own accord. Yes, he thought, there were some com-
pensations to be had from a provincial command.

Wesley, trying not to inhale, walked with his business partner,
Gerald Brockway, co-owner of B.B. Radio Cars, through the
humid fug of the "bullpen" toward the front door. There were
three drivers there waiting for jobs and naturally they were
talking about cars.

"How's the Carlton, Tone," Gerald asked.

"Magic."

"Brilliant."

"Cheers."

Outside, Wesley opened the passenger door of his Rover
for Gerald.

"You happy with this?" Gerald asked. "I thought you
wanted an Orion."

"It's fine," Wesley said.

"Noël got five grand for his Granada."

"Really?"

"They hold their value, the old ones. Amazing. Years later.
It's well rubbish what they did, restyling like that."

Wesley couldn't think of what to say. He thought a shrill
ringing had started in his inner ear. Tinnitus. He lived in constant fear of tinnitus.

"Change for the sake of change," Gerald said, slowly, sadly,
shaking his head.

Wesley started the engine and pulled away.

"Look at Saab."

"Sorry?"

"They've had to bring back the 900. You can't give away a
9000."

"Can we talk about something else, Ger?"

Gerald looked at him. "You all right?"

"Of course. Just, you know."

"No prob, my son. Where are we going to eat?"

"Everyone has heard of samba and bossa nova, sure," Wesley said. "But this is another type of music called *chorinho*—not many people know about it. Love it. Play it all the time. I can lend you some CDs."

"I'd like to give him a break, Wes. But something in me says fire the bastard. Why should we help him, Wes? Why? Big error. 'No good deed goes unpunished,' that's my personal philosophy. Is there any way we can turn this down? What the hell is it?"

"*Chorinho.*"

"You cannot diddle major account customers. Two hours' waiting time? I mean, what does he take us for? Couple of merchant bankers?"

"It means 'little cry.' "

"What is this stuff, Wesley? You got any English music?"

Wesley watched Gerald mash his egg mayonnaise into a creamy pulp. He dribbled thin streams of olive oil and vinegar onto the mixture, which he stirred, and then freely sprinkled on pepper and salt.

"That's disgusting," Wesley said. "How am I meant to eat this?" He pointed his knife at his steak.

"I haven't had a steak for two years. You should have my teeth problems, Wesley. You should feel sorry for me, mate."

"I do feel sorry for you. I'd feel more sorry for you if you'd been to a dentist. You *can* be helped, you know. You don't have to suffer. A man of your age. Jesus."

Gerald ate some of his mixture. Wesley looked around for

a waitress and saw Elizabetta, the plump one. She came over, beaming.

"Pint of lager, please. Ger?"

"Large gin and tonic."

Wesley lowered his voice. "Is, um, Margarita in today?" he asked Elizabetta.

"This afternoon she come."

He shifted his shoulders around. Gerald was not listening. "Tell her I'll phone. Say Wesley will phone. Wesley."

"Wesley. OK."

Gerald pulped his apple crumble with the back of his spoon.

"Nice little place this, Wes. Worth the drive. What is it, Italian?"

"Sort of. Bit of everything."

" 'International cuisine,' then."

Wesley looked around the Caravelle. There was no nautical theme visible in its pragmatic decor, unless you counted the one seascape among its five reproductions on the wall. He and Gerald sat in a row of booths reminiscent more of— what was the word? Seating arrangements in libraries . . . —carrels, yes. Maybe the name was a malapropism, he thought. An asparagus on the banks of the Nile. Someone had blundered: it should have been called the Carrel Café & Restaurant. Names, again . . . He stopped thinking about it and thought instead about Margarita.

Mar-ga-ri-ta. Not Margaret.

He rolled the "r"s. Marrrrgarrrita.

She was dark, of course, very Latin, with a severe thin face that possessed, he thought, what you might call a strong beauty. Not pretty, exactly, but there was a look about her that attracted him, although, he realized, she was one of these southern European women who would not age well. But now she was young and slim and her hair was long and, most important of all, she was Portuguese. *Uma moça bonita.*

Gerald offered him one of his small cigars.

Dr. Liceu Lobo put down his coffee cup and relit his *real excelente.* He drew, with pedantic and practiced care, a steady thin stream of smoke from the neatly docked and already nicely moist end and held it in his mouth, savoring the tobacco's dry tang before pluming it at the small sunbird that pecked at the crumbs of his pastry on the patio table. The bird flew off with a shrill *shgrreakakak* and Dr. Liceu Lobo chuckled. It was time to return to the clinic, Senhora Fontenova was due for her vitamin D injections.

He felt Adalgisa's hand on his shoulder and he leaned his head back against her firm midriff, her finger trickled down over his collarbone and tangled and twirled the dense gray hairs on his chest.

"Your mother wants to see you."

Wesley swung open the gate to his small and scruffy garden and reminded himself yet again to do something about the clematis that overburdened the trellis on either side of his front door. Pauline was bloody meant to be i.c. garden, he told himself, irritated at her, but then he also remembered he had contrived to keep her away from the house the last month or so, prepared to spend weekends and the odd night at her small flat rather than have her in his home. As he hooked his door keys out of his tight pocket with one hand he tugged with the other at a frond of clematis that dangled annoyingly close to his face, and a fine confetti of dust and dead leaves fell quickly onto his hair and shoulders.

After he had showered he lay naked on his bed, his hand on

his cock, and thought about masturbating but decided against. He felt clean and, for the first time that day, almost relaxed. He thought about Margarita and wondered what she looked like with her clothes off. She was thin, perhaps a little on the thin side for his taste, if he were honest, but she did have a distinct bust and her long straight hair was always clean, though he wished she wouldn't tuck it behind her ears and drag it taut into a lank swishing ponytail. Restaurant regulations, he supposed. He realized then that he had never seen her with her hair down and felt, for a moment, a sharp intense sorrow for himself and his lot in life. He sat up and swung his legs off the bed, amazed that there was a shimmer of tears in his eyes.

"God. Jesus!" he said mockingly to himself, out loud. "Poor little chap."

He dressed himself brusquely.

Downstairs, he poured himself a large rum and coke and put Milton Nascimento on the CD player and hummed along to the great man's ethereal falsetto. Never failed to cheer him up. Never failed. He took a great gulp of the chilled drink and felt the alcohol surge. He swayed over to the drinks cabinet and added another slug. It was only four-thirty in the afternoon. Fuck it, he thought. Fuck it.

He should have parked somewhere else, he realized crossly, as unexpected sun warmed the Rover while he waited outside Pauline's bank. He didn't have a headache but his palate was dry and stretched and his sinuses were responding unhappily to the rum. He flared his nostrils and exhaled into his cupped hand. His breath felt unnaturally hot on his palm. He sneezed, three times, violently. Come on, Pauline. Jesus.

She emerged from the stout teak doors of the bank, waved and skittered over toward the car. High heels, he saw. She *has* got nice legs. Definitely, he thought. Thin ankles. They must

be three-inch heels, he reckoned, she'll be taller than me. Was
it his imagination or was that the sun flashing off the small di-
amond cluster of her engagement ring?

He leaned across the seat and flung the door open for her.

"Wesley! You going to a funeral or something? Gaw!"

"It's just a suit. Jesus."

"It's a black suit. Black. Really."

"Charcoal gray."

"Where's your Prince of Wales check? I love that one."

"Cleaners."

"You don't wear a black suit to a christening, Wesley. Honestly."

Professor Liceu Lobo kissed the top of his mother's head and
sat down at her feet.

"Hey, little Mama, how are you today?"

"Oh, I'm fine. A little closer to God."

"Nah, little Mama, He needs you here, to look after me."

She laughed softly and smoothed the hair back from his
forehead in gentle combing motions.

"Are you going to the university today?"

"Tomorrow. Today is for you, little Mama."

He felt her small rough hands on his skin at the hairline
and closed his eyes. His mother had been doing this to him
ever since he could remember. Soothing, like waves on the
shore. "Like waves on the shore your hands on my hair" . . .
The line came to him and with it, elusively, a hint of something more. Don't force it, he told himself, it will come. The
rhythm was fixed already. Like waves on the shore. The
mother figure, mother earth . . . Maybe there was an idea to
investigate. He would work on it in the study, after dinner.
Perhaps a poem? Or maybe the title of a novel? *As ondas em la
praia*. It had a serene yet epic ring to it.

He heard a sound and looked up, opening his eyes to see

Marialva carrying a tray. The muffled belling of ice in a glass jug filled with a clear fruit punch. Seven glasses. The children must be back from school.

Wesley looked across the room at Pauline trying vainly to calm the puce, wailing baby. Daniel-Ian Young, his nephew. It was a better name than Wesley Bright, he thought—just—though he had never come across the two Christian names thus conjoined before. Bit of a mouthful. He wondered if he dared point out to his brother-in-law the good decade-odd remorseless bullying that lay ahead for the youngster once his peers discovered what his initials spelled. He decided to store it away in his grudge-bunker as potential retaliation. Sometimes Dermot really got on his wick.

He watched his brother-in-law, Dermot Young, approach, two pint-tankards in hand. Wesley accepted his gladly. He had a terrible thirst.

"Fine pair of lungs on him, any road," Dermot said. "You were saying, Wesley."

"—No, it's a state called Minas Gerais, quite remote, but with this amazing musical tradition. I mean, you've got Beto Guedes, Toninho Horta, the one and only Milton Nascimento, of course, Lo Borges, Wagner Tiso. All these incredible talents who—"

"—HELEN! Can you put him down, or something? We can't hear ourselves think, here."

Wesley gulped fizzy beer. Pauline, relieved of Daniel-Ian, was coming over with a slice of christening cake on a plate, his mother in tow.

"All right, all right," Pauline said, with an unpleasant leering tone to her voice, Wesley thought. "What are you two plotting? Mmm?"

"Where did you get that suit, Wesley?" his mother asked, guilelessly. "Is it one of your dad's?"

There was merry laughter at this. Wesley kept a smile on his face.

"No," Dermot said. "Wes was telling me about this bunch of musicians from—"

"—Brazil." Pauline's shoulders sagged and she turned wearily to Wesley's mother. "Told you, didn't I, Isobel? Brazil. Brazil. Told you. Honestly."

"You and Brazil," his mother admonished. "It's not as if we've got any Brazilians in the family."

"Not as if you've even been there," Pauline said, a distinct hostility in her voice. "Never even set foot."

Wesley silently hummed the melody from a João Gilberto samba to himself. Gilberto had taken the traditional form and distilled it through a good jazz filter. It was João who had stripped away the excess of percussion in Brazilian music and brought bossa nova to the—

"Yeah, what is it with you and Brazil, Wes?" Dermot asked, a thin line of beer suds on his top lip. "What gives?"

WHUCHINNNNNNG! WHACHANNNNGGG!! Liceu Lobo put down his guitar, and before selecting the mandolin he tied his dreadlocks back behind his head in a slack bun. Gibson Piaçava played a dull roll on the *zabumba* and Liceu Lobo began slowly to strum the musical phrase that seemed to be dominating "The Waves on the Shore" at this stage in its extemporized composition. Joel Carlos Brandt automatically started to echo the mandolin phrases on his guitar and Bola da Rocha plaintively picked up the melody on his saxophone.

Behind the glass of the recording studio Albertina swayed her hips to and fro to the sinuous rhythm that was slowly building. Pure *chorinho*, she thought, sensuous yet melancholy, only Liceu is capable of this, of all the great *choros* in Brazil, he was the greatest. At that moment he looked around and caught her eye and he smiled at her as he played. She kissed the tip of her forefinger and pressed it against the warm glass of the window that separated them. Once Liceu and his fellow musicians started a session like this it could last for days, weeks even. She would wait patiently for him, though, wait until he was finished and take him home to their wide bed.

Wesley stepped out into the back garden and flipped open his mobile phone.

"Café Caravelle, may I help you, please?"

"Ah. Could I speak to, ah, Margarita?"

"MARGARITA! *Telefono.*"

In the chilly dusk of a back garden in Hounslow, Wesley Bright listened to the gabble of foreign voices, the erratic percussion of silverware and china and felt he was calling some distant land, far overseas. A warmth located itself in his body, a spreading coin of heat, deep in his bowels.

"Ghello?" That slight guttural catch on the "h" . . .

"Margarita, it's Wesley."

"Ghello?"

"Wesley. It's me—Wesley."

"Please?"

"WESLEY!" He stopped himself from shouting louder in time, and repeated his name in a throat-tearing whisper several times, glancing around at the yellow windows of Dermot's house. He saw someone peering at him, in silhouette.

"Ah, Wesley," Margarita said. "Yes?"

"I'll pick you up at ten, outside the café."

Pauline stood at the kitchen door, frowning out into the thickening dusk of the garden. Wesley advanced into the rectangle of light the open door had thrown on the grass.

"What're you up to, Wesley?"

Wesley slid his thin phone into his hip pocket.

"Needed a breath of fresh air," he said. "I'm feeling a bit off, to tell the truth. Those vol-au-vents tasted dodgy to me."

Pauline was upset, she had been expecting a meal out after the christening, but she was also concerned for him and his health. "I thought you looked a bit sort of pallid," she said when he dropped her at her flat. She made him wait while she went inside and reemerged with two sachets of mint infusion, "to help settle your stomach," she said. She took them whenever she felt bilious, she told him, and they worked wonders.

As he drove off he smelled strongly the pungent impress of her perfume, or powder or makeup, on his cheek where she had kissed him, and he felt a squirm of guilt at his duplicity— if something so easily accomplished merited the description—and a small pelt of shame covered him for a minute or two as he headed east toward the Café Caravelle and the waiting Margarita.

Her hair was down. Her hair was down and he was both rapt and astonished at the change it wrought in her. And to see her out of black too, he thought, it was almost too much. He carried their drinks through the jostling noisy pub to the back where she sat, on a high stool, elbow resting on a narrow shelf designed to take glasses. She was drinking a double vodka and water, no ice and no slice, a fact he found exciting and vaguely troubling. He had smelled her drink as the barmaid had served up his rum and coke and it had seemed redolent of heavy industry, some strange fuel or new lubricant, something one would pour into a machine rather than down one's throat. It seemed, also, definitely not a drink of the warm South either, not at all apt for his taciturn Latin beauty, more suited to the bleak cravings of a sheet-metal worker in Smolensk. Still, it was gratifying to observe how she put it away, shudderless, in three pragmatic drafts. Then she spoke briefly, brutally, of how much she hated her job. It was a familiar theme, one Wesley recognized from his two previous social encounters with Margarita—the first a snatched coffee in a hamburger franchise before her evening shift began, and then a more leisurely autumnal Sunday lunch at a brash pub on the river at Richmond.

On that last occasion she had seemed out of sorts, cowed perhaps by the strapping conviviality of the tall, noisy lads and their feisty, jolly girls. But tonight she had returned to the same tiresome plaint—the mendacious and rebarbative qualities of the Caravelle's manager, João—so Wesley had to concede it was clearly something of an obsession.

They had kissed briefly and not very satisfactorily after their Sunday pub tryst, and Wesley felt this allowed him now to take her free hand (her other held her cigarette) and squeeze it. She stopped talking and, he thought, half smiled at him.

"Weseley," she said, and stubbed out her cigarette. Then she grinned. "Tonight, I thin I wan to be drunk . . ."

There you had it, he thought. There. That was it. That moment held the gigantic difference between a Pauline and a Margarita. A mint infusion and an iceless vodka. He felt his bowels weaken with shocking desire.

He returned to the bar to fetch another drink for her and ordered the same for himself. The tepid alcohol seemed all the more powerful for the absence of chill. His nasal passages burned, he wrinkled his tear-flooded eyes. Made from potatoes, hard to believe. Or is it potato peelings? His teeth felt loose. He stood beside her. Someone had taken his stool.

Margarita sipped her drink with more decorum this time. "I hate that fockin' job," she said.

He raised her knuckles to his lips and dabbed at them.

"God, I've missed you," he said, then took a deep breath. "Margarita," he said softly, *"tenho muito atração para tu."* He hoped to God he had it right, with the correct slushing and nasal sounds. He found Portuguese farcically difficult to pronounce, no matter how many hours he spent listening to his tapes.

She frowned. Too fast you fool, you bloody fool.

"What?" Her lips half formed a word. "I, I don't—"

More slowly, more carefully: *"Tenho muito atração—muito, muito—para tu."*

He slipped his hand around her thin back, fingers snagging momentarily on the buckle of her bra and drew her to him. He kissed her, there in the hot pub, boldly, with noticeable teeth clash, but no recoil from Margarita.

He moved his head back, his palm still resting on her body, warm above her hip.

She touched her lips with the palp of her thumb, scrutinizing him, not hostile, he was glad to see, not even surprised. She drank some more of her flat gray drink, still looking at him over the rim of her glass.

"Sempre para tu, Margarita, sempre." Huskily, this. Sincere.

"Weseley. What are you saying? *Sempre,* I know. But the rest . . ."

"I . . . I am speaking Portuguese."

"For why?"

"Because, I— Because I want to speak your language to you. I love your language, you must understand. I love it. I hear it in my head in your music."

"Well . . ." She shrugged and reached for her cigarettes. "Then you must not speak Portuguese at me, Weseley. I am Italian."

Marta shucked off her brassiere and had hooked down her panties with her thumbs within seconds, Liceu Lobo thought, of his entering her room in the bordello. He caught a glimpse of her plump fanny from the light cast by the bathroom cubicle. She was hot tonight, on fire, he thought, as he hauled off his T-shirt and allowed his shorts to fall to the floor. As he reached the bedside he felt her hands reaching for his engorged member. He was a pretty boy and even the oldest hooker liked a pretty boy with a precocious and impatient tool. He felt Marta's hands all over his *pepino*, as if she were assessing it for some strumpet's inventory. *Maldito seja!* Liceu Lobo thought, violently clenching his sphincter muscles as Marta settled him between her generous and welcoming thighs, he should definitely have jerked off before coming here tonight. Marta always had that effect on him. *Deus!* He hurled himself into the fray.

It had not gone well. No. He had to face up to that, acknowledge it, squarely. As lovemaking went it was indubitably B minus. B double-minus, possibly. And it was his fault. But could he put it down to the fact that he had been in bed with an Italian girl and *not* a Portuguese one? Or perhaps it had something to do with the half dozen vodkas and water he had consumed as he kept pace with Margarita? . . .

But the mood had changed, subtly, when he had learned the truth, a kind of keening sadness, a thin draft of melancholy seemed to enter the boisterous pub, depressing him. An unmistakable sense of being let down by Margarita's nationality. She was meant to be Portuguese, that was the whole point, anything else was wrong.

He turned over in his bed and stared at the faint silhouette of Margarita's profile as she slept beside him. Did it matter? he urged himself. This was the first non-British girl he had kissed, let alone made love to, so why had he been unable to shake off that sense of distraction? It was a sullenness of spirit that had possessed him, as if he were a spoiled child who had been promised and then denied a present. It was hardly Margarita's fault, after all, but an irrational side of him still blamed her for not being Portuguese, for unconsciously raising his hopes by not warning him from their first encounter that she didn't fit his national bill. Somehow she had to share the responsibility.

He turned away and dozed, and half dreamed of Liceu Lobo in a white suit. On a mountaintop with Leonor or Branca or Caterina or Joana. A balcony with two cane chairs. Mangos big as rugby balls. Liceu, blond hair flying, putting down his guitar, offering his hand, saying, "My deal is my smile." Joana's slim mulatto body. The sound of distant water falling.

He half sat, blinking stupidly.

"Joana?"

The naked figure in his doorway froze.

"Joana?"

The figure moved.

"*Vaffanculo,*" Margarita said, weariness making her voice harsh. She switched on the light and began to get dressed, still talking, but more to herself than to him. Wesley's meager Portuguese was no help here, but he could tell her words were unkind. He hadn't fully awakened from his dream. How could he explain that to her? She was dressed in a moment and did not shut the door as she left.

After she had gone, Wesley pulled on his dressing gown and walked slowly down the stairs. He sat for a while in his unlit sitting room, swigging directly from the rum bottle, resting it on his knee between mouthfuls, coughing and breathing deeply, wiping his mouth with the back of his hand. Eventually he rose to his feet and slid Elis Regina into his CD player.

The strange and almost insupportable plangency of the woman's voice filled the shadowy space around him. *Nem uma lágrima.* "Not one tear," Wesley said to himself. Out loud. His voice sounded peculiar to him, a stranger's. Poor tragic Elis, Elis Regina, who died in 1982, aged thirty-seven, tragically, of an unwise cocktail of drugs and alcohol. "Drink 'n' drugs," the CD's sleeve notes had said. Tragic. A tragic loss to Brazilian music. Fucking tragic. He would call Pauline in the morning, that's what he would do. In the meantime he had his *chorinho* to console him. He would make it up with Pauline, she deserved a treat, some sort of treat, definitely, a weekend somewhere. Definitely. Not one tear, Elis Regina sang for him. He would be all right. There was always Brazil. Not one tear.

The Dream Lover

N ONE OF THESE girls is French, right?"

"No. But they're European."

"Not the same thing, man. French is crucial."

"Of course . . ." I don't know what he is talking about but it seems politic to agree.

"You know any French girls?"

"Of course," I say again. This is almost a lie, but it doesn't matter at this stage.

"But *well*? I mean well enough to ask out?"

"I don't see why not." Now this time we are well into mendacity, but I am unconcerned. I feel good, adult, quite confident today. This lie can germinate and grow for a while.

I am standing in a pale parallelogram of March sunshine, leaning against a wall, talking to my American friend, Preston. The wall belongs to the Centre Universitaire Mediterranéen, a large stuccoed villa on the front at Nice. In front of us is a small cobbled courtyard bounded by a balustrade. Beyond is the Promenade des Anglais, its four lanes busy with Nice's traffic. Over the burnished roofs of the cars I can see the Mediterranean. The Baie des Anges looks gray and grim in this season: old, tired water—ashy, cindery.

"We got to do something . . ." Preston says, a hint of petulant desperation in his voice. I like the "we." Preston scratches his short hard hair noisily. "What with the new apartment and all."

"You moved out of the hotel?"

"Yeah. Want to come by tonight?" He shifts his big frame as if troubled by a fugitive itch, and pats his pockets—breast, hip, thigh—looking for his cigarettes. "We got a bar on the roof."

I am intrigued, but I explain that the invitation has to be turned down as it is a Monday, and every Monday night I have a dinner appointment with a French family—friends of friends of my mother's.

Preston shrugs, then finds and sets fire to a cigarette. He smokes an American brand called "Merit." When he came to France he brought a hundred packs with him. He has never smoked anything else since he was fourteen, he insists.

We watch our fellow students saunter into the building. They are nearly all strangers to me, these bright boys and girls, as I have been in Nice only a few weeks, and so far, Preston is the only friend I have made. Slightly envious of their easy conviviality, I watch the others chatter and mingle—Germans, Scandinavians, Italians, Tunisians, Nigerians . . . We are all foreigners, trying hard to learn French and win our diplomas . . . Except for Preston, who makes no effort at all and seems quite content to remain monoglot.

A young guy with long hair rides his motorbike into the courtyard. He is wearing no shirt. He is English and, apart from me, the only other English person in the place. He revs his motorbike unnecessarily a few times before parking it and switching it off. He takes a T-shirt out of a saddlebag and nonchalantly pulls it on. I think how I too would like to own a motorbike and do exactly what he has done . . . His name is Tim. One day, I imagine, we might be friends. We'll see.

Monsieur Cambrai welcomes me with his usual exhausting, impossible geniality. He shakes my hand fervently and shouts to his wife over his shoulder.

"*Ne bouge pas. C'est l'habitué!*"

That's what he calls me—*l'habitué*. *L'habitué de lundi*, to give the appellation in full, so called because I am invited to dinner every Monday night without fail. He almost never uses my proper name and sometimes I find this perpetual alias a little wearing, a little stressful. "*Salut, l'habitué,*" "*Bien mangé, l'habitué?*" "*Encore du vin, l'habitué?*" and so on. But I like him and the entire Cambrai family; in fact I like them so much that it makes me feel weak, insufficient, cowed.

Monsieur and Madame are small people, fit, sophisticated and nimble, with neat spry figures. Both of them are dentists, it so happens, who teach at the big medical school here in Nice. A significant portion of my affection for them is owing to the fact that they have three daughters—Delphine, Stéphane and Annique—all older than me and all possessed of—to my fogged and blurry eyes—an incandescent, almost supernatural beauty. Stéphane and Annique still live with their parents; Delphine has a flat somewhere in the city, but she often dines at home. These are the French girls that I claimed to know, though "know" is far too inadequate a word to sum up the complexity of my feelings for them. I come to their house on Monday nights as a supplicant and votary, both frightened and in awe of them. I sit in their luminous presence, quiet and eager, for two hours or so, unmanned by my astonishing good fortune.

I am humbled further when I consider the family's disarming, disinterested kindness. When I arrived in Nice they were the only contacts I had in the city, and at my mother's urging, I duly wrote to them citing our tenuous connection via my mother's friends. To my surprise I was promptly invited to dinner and then invited back every Monday night. What shamed me was that I knew I myself could never be so hospitable so quickly, not even to a close friend, and what was more, I knew no one else who would be, either. So I cross the Cambrai threshold each Monday with a rich cocktail of emotions gurgling inside me: shame, guilt, gratitude, admiration and—it goes without saying—lust.

Preston's new address is on the Promenade des Anglais itself—the "Résidence Les Anges." I stand outside the building, looking up, impressed. I have passed it many times before, a distressing and vulgar edifice on this celebrated boulevard, an unadorned rectangle of coppery, smoked glass with stacked ranks of gilded aluminum balconies.

I press a buzzer in a slim, freestanding concrete post and speak into a crackling wire grille. When I mention the name "Mr. Fairchild," glass doors part softly and I am admitted to a bare granite lobby where a taciturn man in a tight suit shows me to the lift.

Preston rents a small studio apartment with a bathroom and kitchenette. It is a neat, pastel-colored and efficient module. On the wall are a series of prints of exotic birds: a toucan, a bateleur eagle, something called a blue shrike. As I stand there looking around I think of my own temporary home, my thin room in Madame d'Amico's ancient, dim apartment, and the inefficient and bathless bathroom I have to share with her other lodgers, and a sudden hot envy rinses through me. I half hear Preston enumerating various financial consequences of his tenancy: how much this studio costs a month; the outrageous supplement he had to pay even to rent it in the first place; and how he had been obliged to cash in his return fare to the States (first-class) in order to meet it. He says he has called his father for more money.

We ride up to the roof, six stories above the Promenade. To my vague alarm there is a small swimming pool up here and a large glassed-in cabana—furnished with a bamboo bar and some rattan seats—labeled *Club Les Anges* in neon copperplate. A barman in a short cerise jacket runs this place, a portly, pale-faced fellow with a poor mustache whose name is Serge. Although Preston jokes patronizingly with him it is immediately quite clear to me both that Serge loathes Preston and that Preston is completely unaware of this powerful animus directed against him.

I order a large gin and tonic from Serge and for a shrill palpitating minute I loathe Preston too. I know there are many better examples on offer, of course, but for the time being this shiny building and its accoutrements will do nicely as an approximation of The Good Life for me. And as I sip my sour drink a sour sense of the world's huge unfairness crowds ruthlessly in. Why should this guileless, big American, barely older than me, with his two thousand cigarettes and his cashable first-class air tickets have all *this* . . . while I live in a narrow frowsty room in an old woman's decrepit apartment? My straitened circumstances are caused by a seemingly interminable postal strike in Britain which means money cannot be transferred to my Nice account and I have to husband my financial resources like a neurotic peasant conscious of a hard winter lowering ahead. Where is *my* money, I want to know, *my* exotic bird prints, *my* club, *my* pool? How long will I have to wait before these artifacts become the commonplace of my life? . . . I allow this unpleasant voice to whine and whinge on in my head as we stand on the terrace and admire the view of the bay. One habit I have already learned, even at my age, is not to resist these fervent grudges—give them a loose rein, let them run themselves out, it is always better in the long run.

In fact I am drawn to Preston and want him to be my friend. He is tall and powerfully built—the word "rangy" comes to mind—affable and not particularly intelligent. To my eyes his clothes are so parodically American as to be beyond caricature: pale blue baggy shirts with button-down collars, old khaki trousers short enough to reveal his white-socked ankles and big brown loafers. He has fair, short hair and even, unexceptionable features. He has a gold watch, a Zippo lighter and an ugly ring with a red stone set in it. He told me once, in all candor, in all modesty, that he "played tennis to Davis Cup standard."

I always wondered what he was doing in Nice, studying at the Centre. At first I thought he might be a draftee avoiding the war in Vietnam but I now suspect—based on some hints he has dropped—that he has been sent off to France as an ob-scure punishment of some sort. His family doesn't want him at home: he has done something wrong and these months in Nice are his penance.

But hardly an onerous one, that's for sure: he has no inter-est in his classes—those he can be bothered to take—or in the language and culture of France. He simply has to endure this exile and he will be allowed to go back home, where, I imag-ine, he will resume his soft life of casual privilege and unre-flecting ease once more. He talks a good deal about his eventual return to the States, where he plans to impose his own particular punishment, or extract his own special reward. He says he will force his father to buy him an Aston Martin. His father will have no say in the matter, he remarks with un-typical vehemence and determination. He will have his Aston Martin, and it is the bright promise of this glossy English car that really seems to sustain him through these dog days on the Mediterranean littoral.

Soon I find I am a regular visitor at the Résidence Les Anges, where I go most afternoons after my classes are over. Preston and I sit in the club, or by the pool if it is sunny, and drink. We consume substantial amounts (it all goes on his tab) and consequently I am usually fairly drunk by sunset. Our conversation ranges far and wide, but at some point in every discussion Preston reiterates his desire to meet French girls. If I do indeed know some French girls, he says, why don't I ask them to the club? I reply that I am working on it, and coolly change the subject.

Over the days, steadily I learn more about my American friend. He is an only child. His father (who has not responded to his requests for money) is a millionaire—real estate. His mother divorced him recently to marry another, richer millionaire. Between his two sets of millionaire parents Preston has a choice of eight homes to visit in and around the USA: in Miami, New York, Palm Springs and a ranch in Montana. Preston dropped out of college after two semesters and does not work.

"Why should I?" he argues reasonably. "They've got more than enough money for me too. Why should I bust my ass working trying to earn more?"

"But isn't it . . . What do you do all day?"

"All kinds of shit . . . But mostly I like to play tennis a lot. And I like to fuck, of course."

"So why did you come to Nice?"

He grins. "I was a bad boy." He slaps his wrist and laughs. "Naughty, naughty Preston."

He won't tell me what he did.

It is Spring in Nice. Each day we start to enjoy a little more sunshine, and whenever it appears, within ten minutes there is a particular girl, lying on the *plage publique* in front of the

Centre, sunbathing. Often I stand and watch her spread out there, still, supine, on the cool pebbles—the only sunbather along the entire bay. It turns out she is well known, that this is a phenomenon that occurs every year. By early summer her tan is solidly established and she is very brown indeed. By August she is virtually black, with that kind of dense, matte tan, the life burned out of the skin, her pores brimming with melanin. Her ambition each year, they say, is to be the brownest girl on the Côte d'Azur . . .

I watch her lying there, immobile beneath the iridescent rain of ultraviolet. It is definitely not warm—even in my jacket and scarf I shiver slightly in the fresh breeze. How can she be bothered? I wonder, but at the same time I have to admit there is something admirable in such single-mindedness, such ludicrous dedication.

Eventually I take my first girl to the Club to meet Preston. Her name is Ingrid, she is in my class, a Norwegian, but with dark auburn hair. I don't know her well but she seems a friendly, uncomplicated soul. She speaks perfect English and German.

"Are you French?" Preston asks, almost immediately.

Ingrid is very amused by this. "I'm Norwegian," she explains. "Is it important?"

I apologize to Preston when Ingrid goes off to change into her swimming costume, but he waves it away, not to worry, he says, she's cute. Ingrid returns and we sit in the sun and order the first of our many drinks. Ingrid, after some prompting, smokes one of Preston's Merit cigarettes. The small flaw that emerges to mar our pleasant afternoon is that the more Ingrid drinks, the more her conversation becomes increasingly dominated by references to a French boy she is seeing called Jean-Jacques. Preston hides his disappointment; he is the acme of good manners.

Later we play poker using cheese biscuits as chips. Ingrid sits opposite me in her multicolored swimsuit. She is plumper than I had imagined, and I decide that if I had to sum her up in one word it would be "homely." Except for one detail: she has very hairy armpits. On one occasion she sits back in her chair, studying her cards for a full minute, her free hand idly scratching a bite on the back of her neck. Both Preston's and my eyes are drawn to the thick divot of auburn hair that is revealed by this gesture: we stare at it, fascinated, as Ingrid deliberates whether to call or raise.

After she has gone Preston confesses that he found her unshavenness quite erotic. I am not so sure.

That night we sit in the Club long into the night, as usual the place's sole customers, with Serge unsmilingly replenishing our drinks as Preston calls for them. Ingrid's presence, the unwitting erotic charge that she has detonated in our normally tranquil, bibulous afternoons, seems to have unsettled and troubled Preston somewhat, and without any serious prompting on my part he tells me why he has come to Nice. He informs me that the man his mother remarried was a widower, an older man, with four children already in their twenties. When Preston dropped out of college he went to stay with his mother and new stepfather.

He exhales, he eats several olives, his face goes serious and solemn for a moment.

"This man, Michael, had three daughters—and a son, who was already married—and, man, you should have seen those girls." He grins, a stupid, gormless grin. "I was eighteen years old and I got three beautiful girls sleeping down the corridor from me. What am I supposed to do?"

The answer, unvoiced, seemed to slip into the Club like a draft of air. I felt my spine tauten.

"You mean—?"

"Yeah, sure."

I didn't want to speak, so I think through this. I imagine a big silent house, night, long dark corridors, closed doors. Three bored blond tanned stepsisters. Suddenly there's a tall young man in the house, a virtual stranger, who plays tennis to Davis Cup standard.

"What went wrong?" I manage.

"Oldest one, Janie, got pregnant, didn't she? Last year."

"Abortion?"

"Are you kidding? She just married her fiancé real fast."

"You mean she was engaged when—"

"He doesn't know a thing. But she told my mother."

"The, the child was—"

"Haven't seen him yet." He turns and calls for Serge. "No one knows for sure, no one suspects . . ." He grins again. "Let's hope the kid doesn't start smoking Merits." He reflects on his life a moment, and turns his big mild face to me. "That's why I'm here. Keeping my head down. Not exactly flavor-of-the-month back home."

The next girl I take to the Club is also a Scandinavian—we have eight in our class—but this time a Swede, called Danni. Danni is very attractive and vivacious, in my opinion, with straight white-blond hair. She's a tall girl, and she would be perfect but for the fact that she has one slightly withered leg, noticeably thinner than the other, which causes her to limp. She is admirably unself-conscious about her disability.

"Hi," Preston says. "Are you French?"

Danni hides her incredulity. *"Mais oui, monsieur. Bien sûr."* Like Ingrid, she finds this presumption highly amusing. Preston soon realizes his mistake and makes light of his disappointment.

Danni wears a small cobalt bikini and even swims in the pool, which is freezing. (Serge says there is something wrong with the heating mechanism but we don't believe him.)

Danni's fortitude impresses Preston: I can see it in his eyes as he watches her dry herself. He asks her what happened to her leg and she tells him she had polio as a child.

"Shit, you were lucky you don't need a caliper."

This breaks the ice and we soon get noisily drunk, much to Serge's irritation. But there is little he can do, as there is no one else in the Club who might complain. Danni produces some grass and we blatantly smoke a joint. Typically, apart from faint nausea, the drug has not the slightest effect on me, but it affords Serge a chance to be officious, and as he clears away a round of empty glasses he says to Preston, "*Ça va pas, monsieur, non, non, ça va pas.*"

"Fuck you, Serge," he says amiably, and Danni's unstoppable blurt of laughter sets us all off. I sense Serge's humiliation and realize the relationship with Preston is changing fast: the truculent deference has gone; the dislike is overt, almost a challenge.

After Danni has left, Preston tells me about his latest money problems. His bar bill at the Club now stands at over four hundred dollars and the management is insisting it be settled. His father won't return his calls or acknowledge telegrams and Preston has no credit cards. He is contemplating pawning his watch in order to pay something into the account and defer suspicion. I buy it off him for five hundred francs.

I look around my class counting the girls I know. I know most of them by now, well enough to talk to. Both Ingrid and Danni have been back to the Club and have enthused about their afternoons there, and I realize that to my fellow students I have become an object of some curiosity as a result of my unexpected ability to dispense these small doses of luxury and decadence: the exclusive address, the privacy of the Club, the pool on the roof, the endless flow of free drinks . . .

Preston decided to abandon his French classes a while ago and I am now his sole link with the Centre. It is with some mixed emotions—I feel vaguely pimplike, oddly smirched—that I realize how simple it is to attract girls to the Club Les Anges.

Annique Cambrai is the youngest of the Cambrai daughters and the closest to me in age. She is only two years older than me but seems considerably more than that. I was, I confess, oddly daunted by her mature good looks, dark with a lean attractive face, and because of this at first I think she found me rather aloof, but now, after many Monday dinners, we have become more relaxed and friendly. She is studying law at the University of Nice and speaks good English with a marked American accent. When I comment on this she explains that most French universities now offer you a choice of accents when you study English and, like 90 percent of students, she has chosen American.

I see my opportunity and take it immediately: would she, I diffidently inquire, like to come to the Résidence Les Anges to meet an American friend of mine and perhaps try her new accent out on him?

The next morning, on my way down the rue de France to the Centre, I see Preston standing outside a pharmacy reading the *Herald Tribune*. I call his name and cross the road to tell him the excellent news about Annique.

"You won't believe this," I say, "but I finally got a real French girl."

Preston's face looks odd: half a smile, half a morose grimace of disappointment.

"That's great," he says dully, "wonderful."

A tall, slim girl steps out of the pharmacy and hands him a plastic bag.

"This is Lois," he says. We shake hands.

I know who Lois is, Preston has often spoken of her: my damn-near fiancée, he calls her. It transpires that Lois has flown over spontaneously and unannounced to visit him. "And, boy, are my mom and dad mad as hell," she says, laughing.

Lois is a pretty girl, with a round, innocent face quite free of makeup. She is tall—even in her sneakers she is as tall as me—with a head of incredibly thick, dense brown hair which, for some reason, I associate particularly with American girls. I feel sure also, though as yet I have no evidence, that she is a very clean person—physically clean, I mean to say—someone who showers and washes regularly, smelling of soap and the lingering farinaceous odor of talcum powder.

I stroll back with them to the Résidence. Lois's arrival has temporarily solved Preston's money problems: they have cashed in her return ticket and paid off the bar bill and the next quarter's rent that had come due. Preston feels rich enough to buy back his watch from me.

Annique looks less mature and daunting in her swimsuit, I'm pleased to say, though I was disappointed that she favored a demure apple-green one-piece. The pool's heater has been "fixed" and for the first time we all swim in the small azure rectangle—Preston and Lois, Annique and me. It is both strange and exciting for me to see Annique so comparatively unclothed and even stranger to lie side by side, thigh by thigh, inches apart, sunbathing.

Lois obviously assumes Annique and I are a couple—a quite natural assumption under the circumstances, I suppose—she would never imagine I had brought her for Preston. I keep catching him gazing at Annique, and a mood of frustration and intense sadness seems to emanate from him—

a mood of which only I am aware. And in turn a peculiar exhilaration builds inside me, not just because of Lois's innocent assumption about my relation to Annique, but also because I know now that I have succeeded. I have brought Preston the perfect French girl: Annique, by his standards, represents the paradigm, the Platonic ideal for this American male. Here she is, unclothed, lying by his pool, in his club, drinking his drinks, but he can do nothing—and what makes my own excitement grow is the realization that for the first time in our friendship—perhaps for the first time in his life—Preston envies another person. Me.

As this knowledge dawns, so too does my impossible love for Annique. Impossible, because nothing will ever happen. I know that—but Preston doesn't, and somehow that ghostly love affair, our love affair, Annique and me, that will carry on in Preston's head, in his hot and tormented imagination, embellished and elaborated by his disappointment and sense of lost opportunity, will be more than enough, more than I could ever have hoped for.

Now that Lois has arrived I stay away from the Résidence Les Anges. It won't be the same again and, despite my secret delight, I don't want to taunt Preston with the spectre of Annique. But I find that without the spur of his envy the tender fantasy inevitably dims; in order for my dream life, my dream love, to flourish, I need to share it with Preston. I decide to pay a visit. Preston opens the door of his studio.

"Hi, stranger," he says with some enthusiasm. "Am I glad to see you." He seems sincere. I follow him into the apartment. The small room is untidy, the bed unmade, the floor strewn with female clothes. I hear the noise of the shower from the bathroom: Lois may be a clean person but it is clear she is also something of a slut.

"How are things with Annique?" he asks, almost at once, as casually as he can manage. He has to ask, I know it.

I look at him. "Good." I let the pause develop, pregnant with innuendo. "No, they're good."

His nostrils flare and he shakes his head.

"God, you're one lucky—"

Lois comes in from the bathroom in a dressing gown, toweling her thick hair dry.

"Hi, Edward," she says, "what's new?" Then she sits down on the bed and begins to weep.

We stand and look at her as she sobs quietly.

"It's nothing," Preston says. "She just wants to go home." He tells me that neither of them has left the building for eight days. They are completely, literally, penniless. Lois's parents have canceled her credit cards, and collect calls home have failed to produce any response. Preston has been unable to locate his father and now his stepfather refuses to speak to him (a worrying sign), and although his mother would like to help she is powerless for the moment, given Preston's fall from grace. Preston and Lois have been living on a diet of olives, peanuts and cheese biscuits served up in the bar and, of course, copious alcohol.

"Yeah, but now we're even banned from there," Lois says, with an unfamiliar edge to her voice.

"Last night I beat up on that fuckwit, Serge," Preston explains with a shrug. "Something I had to do."

He goes on to enumerate their other problems: their bar bill stands at over three hundred dollars; Serge is threatening to go to the police unless he is compensated; the management has grown hostile and suspicious.

"We got to get out of here," Lois says miserably. "I hate it here, I hate it."

Preston turns to me. "Can you help us out?" he says. I feel laughter erupt within me.

I stand in Nice station and hand Preston two train tickets to Luxembourg and two one-way Iceland Air tickets to New York. Lois reaches out to touch them as if they were sacred relics.

"You've got a six-hour wait in Reykjavík for your connection," I tell him, "but, believe me, there is no cheaper way to fly."

I bask in their voluble gratitude for a while. They have no luggage with them, as they could not be seen to be quitting the Résidence. Preston says his father is now in New York and assures me I will be reimbursed the day they arrive. I have spent almost everything I possess on these tickets, but I don't care—I am intoxicated with my own generosity and the strange power it has conferred on me. Lois leaves us to go in search of a toilet and Preston embraces me in a clumsy hug. "I won't forget this, man," he says many times. We celebrate our short but intense friendship and affirm its continuance, but all the while I am waiting for him to ask me—I can feel the question growing in his head like a tumor. Through the crowds of passengers we see Lois making her way back. He doesn't have much time left.

"Listen," he begins, his voice low, "did you and Annique . . . ? I mean, are you—"

"We've been looking for an apartment. That's why you haven't seen much of me."

"Jesus . . ."

Lois calls out something about the train timetable, but we are not listening. Preston seems to be trembling, he turns away, and when he turns back I see the pale fires of impotent resentment light his eyes.

I look at him in that way men look at each other. And then I say, "Are you fucking her?"

"Why else would we be looking for an apartment?" Lois arrives and immediately notices Preston's taut face, oddly pinched. "What's going on?" Lois asks. "Are you OK?"

Preston gestures at me, as if he can't pronounce my name. "Annique . . . They're moving in together."

Lois squeals. She's so pleased, she really is, she really really likes Annique.

By the time I see them onto the train Preston has calmed down and our final farewells are sincere. He looks around the modest station intently as if trying to record its essence, as if now he wished to preserve something of this city he inhabited so complacently, with such an absence of curiosity.

"God, it's too bad," he says with an exquisite fervor. "I know I could have liked Nice. I *know*. I really could."

I back off, wordless, this is too good, this is too generous of him. This is perfect.

"Give my love to Annique," Preston says quietly, as Lois calls loud goodbyes.

"Don't worry," I say, looking at Preston. "I will."

Alpes-Maritimes

NNELIESE, ULRICKE AND I go into Steve's sitting room. Steve is sitting at a table writing a letter. "Hi," he says, not looking up. "Won't be a second." He scribbles his name and seals the letter in an envelope as the three of us watch him, wordlessly. He stands up and turns to face us. His long clean hair, brushed straight back from his forehead, falls to his shoulders. Perhaps it's something to do with the dimness of the room but, against the pale ghost of his swimming trunks, his cock seems oddly pigmented—almost brown.

"Make yourselves at home," he says. "I'll just go put some clothes on."

I have a girl now—Ulricke—and so everything should be all right. And it is, I suppose, except that I want Anneliese, her twin sister. I look closely at Anneliese to see her reaction to Steve's nakedness (Steve wants Anneliese too). She and Ulricke smile at each other. They both press their lips together with a hand, their eyes thin with delighted amusement at Steve's eccentricity. Automatically I smile too, but in fact I am covered in a hot shawl of irritation as I recall Steve's long-stride saunter from the room, his calmness, his unconcern.

Bent comes in. He is Steve's flat-mate, a ruddy Swede, be-spectacled, with a square bulging face and unfortunate frizzy hair.

"Does he always do that?" Anneliese asks.

"I'm afraid so," Bent says, ruefully. "He comes in—he removes his clothes."

The girls surrender themselves to their laughter. I ask for a soft drink.

It wasn't easy to meet Ulricke. She and Anneliese were doing a more advanced course than me at the Centre and so our classes seldom coincided. I remember being struck by rare glimpses of this rather strong-looking fashionable girl. I think it was Anneliese that I saw first, but I can't be sure. But the fact is that the one I met was Ulricke. How was I meant to know they were twins? By the time I discovered that those glimpses were not of one and the same person it was too late.

One lunchtime I was walking up to the university restaurant by the Faculté de Droit (the *restauru* by the *fac*, as the French have it) when I heard my name called.

"Edward!" I turned.

It was Henni, a Finnish girl I knew, with Anneliese. At least I thought it was Anneliese but it turned out to be Ulricke. Until you know them both it's very hard to spot the difference.

We had lunch together. Then Ulricke and I went for coffee to a bar called Le Pub Latin. We spoke French, I with some difficulty. There was no mention of a twin sister that first day, no Anneliese. I talked about my father; I lied mod-

estly about my age, with more élan about my ambitions. Soon
Ulricke interrupted to tell me that she spoke very good English. After that it was much easier.

Ulricke: tall, broad-shouldered, with a round, good-complex-
ioned face—though her cheeks and nose tend to develop a
shine as the day wears on—thick straight peanut-colored hair
parted in the middle . . . She and Anneliese are not-quite-
identical twins. To be candid, Anneliese is prettier, though in
compensation Ulricke has the sweeter temperament, as they
say. Recently, Anneliese has streaked her hair blond, which, as
well as distinguishing her from her sister (too late, too late),
adds, in my opinion, dramatically to her attractiveness. In
Bremen, where they live (father a police inspector), they were
both prizewinning gymnasts as youngsters. Ulricke told me
that they ceased entering competitions "after our bosoms
grew," but the strenuous training has left them with the legacy
of sturdy well-developed frames. They are thin-hipped and
broad-shouldered, with abnormally powerful deltoid muscles
that give their figures a tapered manly look.

Steve returns, in pale jeans, sandals and a cheesecloth smock-
shirt he brought back from his last trip to Morocco. He pours
wine for everyone. Steve is a New Zealander, somewhat older
than the rest of us—late twenties, possibly even thirty. He is
very clean, almost obsessive about his cleanliness, always
showering, always attending to the edges of his body—the
calluses on his toes, his teeth, his cuticles. He has a mustache,
a neat blond General Custer affair that curls up at the ends.
It's a similarity—to General Custer—which is amplified by
his wavy shoulder-length brown hair. He has spent several
years traveling the Mediterranean—Rhodes, Turkey, Ibiza,

Hammamet. It's quite likely that he sells drugs to support himself. He's not rich, but he's not poor either. None of us knows where he gets his money. On his return from his last Moroccan trip he had also purchased a mid-calf, butter-colored Afghan coat that I covet. I've known him vaguely since I arrived in Nice, but lately, because of his interest in Anneliese, I tend to see him rather more often than I would wish. Whenever I get the chance I criticize Steve for Anneliese's benefit, but subtly, as if my reservations were merely the result of a disinterested study of human nature. Just before we arrived at the flat I managed to get Anneliese to admit that there was something unappealingly sinister about Steve. Now, when he's out of earshot, we exchange remarks about his nudism. I don't believe the girls find it as offensive as I do.

"I think it's the height of selfishness," I say. "I didn't ask to see his penis."

The girls and Bent laugh.

"I think he's strange," Anneliese says, with a curious expression on her face. I can't tell if she finds this alluring or not.

Ulricke and I continued to see each other. Soon I learned about the existence of Anneliese, duly met her and realized my mistake. But by then I was "associated" with Ulricke. To switch attention to Anneliese would have hurt and offended her sister, and with Ulricke hurt and offended, Anneliese would be bound to take her side. I found myself trapped; both irked and tantalized. I came to see Anneliese almost as often as I saw Ulricke. She appeared to like me—to my deep chagrin we became "friends."

I forced myself to concentrate on Ulricke—to whom I was genuinely attracted—but she was only the shadow on the cave wall, so to speak. Of course I was discreet and tactful: Ulricke—and Anneliese at first—knew nothing of my real desires. But as the bonds between the three of us developed I came to think of other solutions. I realized I could never "possess" Anneliese in the way I did her twin; I could never colonize or settle my real affections in her person with her approval . . . And so I resolved to make her instead a sphere of influence—unilaterally, and without permission, to extend my stewardship and protection over her. If I couldn't have her, then no one else should.

"When ought we to go to Cherry's, do you think?" Bent asks in his precise grammar. We discuss the matter. Cherry is an American girl of iridescent, unreal—and therefore perfectly inert—beauty. She lives in a villa high above the coast at Villefranche which she shares with some other girl students from a college in Ann Arbor, Michigan. They stick closely and rather chastely together, these American girls, as their guileless amiability landed them in trouble when they first arrived in Nice. The Tunisian boys at the Centre would ask them back to their rooms for a cup of coffee, and the girls, being friendly, intrigued to meet foreigners and welcoming the opportunity to practice their execrable French, happily accepted. And then when the Tunisian boys tried to fuck them they were outraged. The baffled Tunisians couldn't understand the tears, the slaps, the threats. Surely, they reasoned, if a girl agrees to have a cup of coffee in your room there is only one thing on her mind? As a result, the girls moved out of Nice to their high villa in Villefranche, where—apart from their classes at the Centre—they spent most of their time, and their French deteriorated beyond redemption. Soon they could only associate with Anglophones and all yearned to return to the USA. They were strange gloomy exiles, these girls, like passengers permanently in transit. The present moment—always the most important—held nothing for them.

Their tenses were either past or future; their moods nostalgia or anticipation. And now one of their number—Cherry—was breaking out, her experiences in Nice having confirmed her in her desire to be a wife. She was returning to marry her be-mused beau, and tonight was her farewell party.

We decided to go along, to make our way to Villefranche. Mild Bent has a car—a VW—but he says he has to detour to pick up his girlfriend. Ulricke announces that she and I will hitchhike. Steve and Anneliese can go with Bent, she says. I want to protest, but say nothing.

Ulricke and Anneliese live in a large converted villa, prewar, up by the Fac de Lettres at Magnan. They rent a large room in a ground-floor flat that belongs to an Uruguayan poet (he teaches Spanish literature at the university) called César.

One night—not long after our first meetings—I'm walking Ulricke home. It's quite late. I promise myself that if we get to the villa after midnight I'll ask if I can stay, as it's a long walk back to my room in the rue Dante down in the city. Depend-able Ulricke invites me in for a cup of coffee. At the back of the flat the windows are at ground level and overlook a gar-den. Ulricke and Anneliese use them as doors to avoid passing through the communal hall. We clamber through the window and into the room. It is big, bare and clean. There are two beds, a bright divan and some wooden chairs that have re-cently been painted a shiny new red. A few cute drawings have been pinned on the wall and there is a single houseplant, flourishing almost indecently from all the attention it re-ceives—the leaves always dark green and glossy, the earth in the pot moist and leveled. The rest of the flat is composed of César's bedroom, his study, a kitchen and bathroom.

We drink our coffee, we talk—idly, amicably. Anneliese is late, out at the cinema with friends. I look at my watch: it is after midnight. I make my request and Ulricke offers me the divan. There is a moment, after we have stripped off the coverlet and tucked in an extra blanket, when we both stand quite close to each other. I lean in her direction, a hand weakly touches her shoulder, we kiss. We sit down on the bed. It is all pleasantly uncomplicated and straightforward.

When Anneliese returns she seems pleased to see me. After more coffee and conversation, the girls change discreetly into their pajamas in the bathroom. While they're gone I undress to my underpants and socks and slide into bed. The girls come back, the lights go out and we exchange cheery *bonsoirs*.

On the hard small divan I lie awake in the dark, Ulricke and Anneliese sleeping in their beds a few feet away. I feel warm, content, secure—like a member of a close and happy family, as if Ulricke and Anneliese were my sisters and beyond the door in the quiet house lay our tender parents . . .

In the morning I meet César. He is thin and febrile, with tousled dry hair. He speaks fast but badly flawed English. We talk about London, where he lived for two years before coming to Nice. Ulricke tells me that as a poet he is really quite famous in Uruguay. Also she tells me that he had an affair with Anneliese when the girls first moved in—but now they're just friends. Unfortunately, this forces a change in my attitude toward César: I like him, but resentment will always distance us now. Whenever he and Anneliese talk I find myself searching for vestiges of their former intimacy—but there seems nothing there anymore.

We all possess, like it or not, the people we know, and are possessed by them in turn. We all own and forge an image of others in our minds which is inviolable and private. We make those private images public at our peril. Revelation is an audacious move to be long pondered. Unfortunately, this impulse occurs when we are least able to control it, when we're distracted by love—or hate . . .

But we can possess others without their ever being truly aware of it. For example, I possess Steve and Anneliese in ways they could never imagine.

I often wonder what Anneliese thinks about while Ulricke and I are fucking across the room from her. Is she irritated? Curious? Happy? The intimacy of our domestic setup causes me some embarrassment at first, but the girls seem quite unperturbed. I affect a similar insouciance. But although we live in such proximity we maintain a bizarrely prim decorum. We don't wander around naked. Ulricke and I undress while Anneliese is in the bathroom, or else with the lights out. I have yet to see Anneliese naked. And she's always with us too—Ulricke and I have never spent a night alone. Since her affair with César she has had no boyfriend. My vague embarrassment swiftly departs and I begin to enjoy Anneliese's presence during the night—like some mute and unbelievably lax chaperone. One day, to my regret, she tells me how happy she is that Ulricke "has" me; how pleased she is that we are together. The twin sisters are typically close; Anneliese is the more self-composed and confident and she feels protective toward Ulricke, who's more vulnerable and easily hurt. I reassure her of my sincerity and try not to let the strain show on my face.

With some dismay I watch Steve—an exotic figure in his Afghan coat and flowing hair—join Anneliese in the back of Bent's VW. Ulricke and I wave them on their way, then we walk down the road from the apartment block toward the Promenade des Anglais. Although it is after nine o'clock the night air is not unpleasantly cool. For the first time the spring chill has left the air—a presage of the bright summer to come. We walk down rue de la Buffa and cut over to the rue de France. The whores in the boutique doorways seem pleased at the clemency of the weather. They call across the street to each other in clear voices; some of them even wear hot pants.

It's not that warm. Ulricke wears a white PVC raincoat and a scarf. I put my arm around her shoulders and hear the crackle of the plastic material. The glow from the streetlamps sets highlights in the shine on her nose and cheeks . . . I worry about Steve and Anneliese in the back of Bent's car.

I begin to spend more and more nights at Ulricke's. Madame d'Amico, my landlady, makes no comment on my prolonged absences. I visit my small room in her flat regularly to change my clothes but I find myself increasingly loath to spend nights alone there. Its fusty smell, its dismal view of the interior courtyard, the dull conversations with my fellow lodgers, depress me. I am happy to have exchanged lonely independence for the hugger-mugger intimacy of the villa. Indeed, for a week or so life there becomes even more cramped. The twins are joined by a girlfriend from Bremen, called Clara—twenty-two, sharp-faced, candid—in disgrace with her parents and spending a month or two visiting friends while waiting for tempers back home to cool. I ask her what she has done. She says she had an affair with her father's business partner and oldest friend. This was discovered, and the ramifications of the scandal spread to the boardroom: suits are being filed, resignations demanded, takeover bids plotted. Clara seems quite calm about it all, her only regret being that her lover's daughter—who hitherto had been her constant companion since childhood—now refuses to see or speak to her. Whole lives are irreparably askew.

Clara occupies the divan. She sleeps naked and is less concerned with privacy than the other girls. I find I relish the dormitory-like aspect of our living arrangements even more. At night I lie docilely beside Ulricke, listening to the three girls talking in German. I can't understand a word—they could be talking about me, for all I know. Clara smokes French cigarettes and their pleasant sour smell lingers in the air after the lights are switched out. Ulricke and I wait for a diplomatic five minutes or so before making love. That fragrance of Gauloises or Gitanes is forever associated with those tense palpitating moments of darkness: Ulricke's warm strong body, the carnal anticipation, the sounds of Clara and Anneliese settling themselves in their beds, their fake yawns.

On the Promenade des Anglais the shiny cars sweep by. Ulricke and I stick out our thumbs, goosing the air. We always get lifts immediately and have freely hitched, usually with Anneliese, the length of the Côte d'Azur, from Saint-Raphaël to Menton, at all hours of the day or night. One warmish evening, near Aix-en-Provence, the three of us decided spontaneously to sleep out in a wood. We huddled up in blankets and awoke at dawn to find ourselves quite soaked with dew.

A car stops. The driver—a man—is going to Monte Carlo. We ask him to take the *haute corniche*. Cherry's villa is perched so high above the town that the walk up from the coast road is exhausting. Ulricke sits in the front—the sex of the driver determines our position. To our surprise we have found that very often single women will stop for the three of us. They are much more generous than the men as a rule: in our travels the women frequently buy us drinks and meals, and once we were given a hundred francs. Something about the three of us prompts this largesse. There is, I feel, something charmed about us as a trio, Ulricke, Anneliese and me. This is why—

quite apart from his rebarbative personal habits—I so resent
Steve. He is an interloper, an intruder: his presence, his interest in Anneliese, threatens me, us. The trio becomes a banal
foursome, or—even worse—two couples.

From the small terrace at Cherry's villa there is a perfect view
of Villefranche and its bay, edged by the bright beads of the
harbor lights and the headlamps of cars on the coast road.
The dim noise of traffic, the sonic rip of some lout's motorbike, drift upward to the villa, competing with the thump and
chords of music from inside. *Crosby, Stills, Nash and Young—
Live, The Yes Album, Hunky Dory* . . . curious how these LPs
pin and fix humdrum moments of our lives—precise as al-
manacs. An *ars brevis* for the quotidian.

The exquisite Cherry patrols her guests, enveloped in a fug
of genial envy from her girlfriends. It's not her impending
marriage that prompts this emotion so much as the prospect
of the "real" Coca-Cola, "real" milk and "real" meat she will
be able to consume a few days hence. The girls from Ann
Arbor reminisce indefatigably about American meals they
have known. To them, France, Nice, is a period of abstention,
a penance for which they will be rewarded in calories and car-
bohydrates when they return home.

I stroll back inside to check on Steve and Anneliese. My
mistake was to have allowed them to travel together in Bent's
car. It conferred an implicit acknowledgment of their "cou-
pledom" on them without Steve having to do anything about
it. Indeed he seems oddly passive with regard to Anneliese, as
if content to bide his time. Perhaps he is a little frightened of
her? Perhaps it's his immense vanity: time itself will impress
upon her the logic and inevitability of their union . . . ? Now
I see him sitting as close to Anneliese as possible, as if adja-
cency alone were sufficient to possess her.

Ulricke talks to Bent's girlfriend, Gudrun, another Scandinavian. We are a polyglot crew at the Centre—almost every European country represented. Tonight you can hear six distinct languages . . . I pour myself a glass of wine from an unlabeled bottle. There is plenty to drink. I had brought a bottle of Martini & Rossi as my farewell present to Cherry but left it in my coat pocket when I saw the quantity of wine on offer.

The wine is cold and rough. Decanted no doubt from some huge barrel in the local *cave*. It is cheap and not very potent. We were drinking this wine the night of my audacity.

César had a party for some of his students in the Spanish Lit course. After strenuous consumption most people had managed to get very drunk. César sang Uruguayan folk songs—perhaps they were his poems, for all I know—to his own inept accompaniment on the guitar. I saw Anneliese collect some empty bottles and leave the room. Moments later I followed. The kitchen was empty. Then from the hall I saw the bathroom door ajar. I pushed it open. Anneliese was reapplying her lipstick.

"I won't be long," she said.

I went up behind her and put my arm around her. The gesture was friendly, fraternal. She leaned back, pursing, pouting and repursing her lips to spread the orange lipstick. We talked at our reflections.

"Good party," I said.

"César may be a poet but he cannot sing."

We laughed, I squeezed. It was all good fun. Then I covered her breasts with my hands. I looked at our reflection: our faces side by side, my hands claws on her chest.

"Anneliese . . ." I began, revealing everything in one word, watching her expression register, interpret, change.

"Hey, tipsy boy," she laughed, clever girl, reaching around to slap my side. "I'm not Ulricke."

We broke apart; I heeled a little, drunkenly. We grinned, friends again. But the moment lay between us, like a secret. Now she knew.

The party is breaking up. People drift away. I look at Steve, he seems to have his arm around Anneliese. Ulricke joins me.

"What's happening?" I ask Steve.

"Cliff's taking us down to the town. He says they may be at the café tonight."

I confirm this with Cliff, who, improbably, is French. He's a dull, inoffensive person who—we have discovered to our surprise—runs drug errands for the many tax-exiled rock musicians who while away their time on the Côte d'Azur. Every now and then these stars and their retinue emerge from the fastnesses of their wired-off villas and patronize a café on the harbor front at Villefranche. People sit around and gawp at the personalities and speculate about the hangers-on—the eerie thugs, the haggard, pale women, the brawling kids.

A dozen of us set off. We stroll down the sloping road as it meanders in a sequence of hairpins down the steep face of the hills to the bright town spangling below. Steve, I notice, is holding hands with Anneliese. I hate the look on his face: king leer. I feel a sudden unbearable anger. What *right* has he got to do this, to sidle into our lives, to take possession of Anneliese's hand in that way?

The four of us and Cliff have dropped back from the others. Cliff, in fractured English, is telling us of his last visit to the rock star's villa. I'm barely listening—something to do with a man and a chicken . . . I look back. Anneliese and Steve have stopped. He removes his Afghan coat and places it capelike around Anneliese's shoulders. He gives a mock-chivalric bow and Anneliese curtsies. These gestures, I recognize with alarm, are the early foundations of a couple's private language—actions, words and shared memories whose mean-

ing and significance only they can interpret and which ex-
clude the world at large. But at the same time they tell me that
nothing intimate—no kiss, no caress—has yet passed between
them. I have only moments left to me.

The other members of our party have left the road and entered a narrow gap between houses which is the entrance to a
thin defile of steps—some hundred yards long—that cuts
down the hill directly to the town below. The steps are steep
and dark with many an illogical angle and turn. From below I
hear the clatter of descending feet and excited cries. Cliff goes
first, Ulricke follows. I crouch to tie a shoelace. Anneliese
passes. I jump up and with the slightest of tussles insinuate
myself between her and Steve.

In the dark cleft of the steps there is just room for two people to pass. I put my hands on the rough iron handrails and
slow my pace. Anneliese skips down behind Ulricke. Steve
bumps at my back. Soon I can barely make out Anneliese's
blond hair.

"Can I get by, please?"

I ignore Steve, although he's treading on my heels. Below
me Anneliese turns a bend out of sight.

"Come *on*, for God's sake."

"Bit tricky in the dark."

Roughly, Steve attempts to wrest my arm from the
handrail. He swears. I stop dead, lock my elbows and brace
myself against his shoving.

"You English fuck!" He punches me quite hard in the back.
I run down the steps to a narrow landing where they make a
turn. I face Steve. He is lean and slightly taller than me, but
I'm not interested in physical prowess, only delay. Farther
down the flights of steps the sound of footfalls grows ever
fainter. I hold the bridge. Steve is panting.

"What do you think you're doing?" he says. "Who do you
think you are? Her father? You don't own these girls, you
know."

He takes a swing at me. I duck my head and his knuckles jar painfully on my skull. Steve lets out a yip of pain. Through photomatic violet light I lunge at him as he massages blood into his numbed fist. With surprising ease I manage to throw him heavily to the ground. At once I turn and spring down the steps. I take them five at a time, my fingertips brushing the handrails like outriggers.

Ulricke and Anneliese are waiting at the bottom. The others have gone on to the harbor front. I seize their hands.

"Quickly," I say. "This way!"

Astonished, the girls run with me, laughing and questioning. We run down back streets. Eventually we stop.

"What happened?" Anneliese asks.

"Steve attacked me," I say. "Suddenly—tried to hit me. I don't know why."

Our feet crunch on the pebbles as we walk along Villefranche's *plage publique*. I pass the Martini bottle to Ulricke, who stops to take a swig. We have discussed Steve and his neuroses for a pleasant hour. At the end of the bay's curve a small green hut is set on the edge of the coast road. It juts out over the beach, where it is supported by thick wooden piles. We settle down here, sheltered by the overhang, spreading Steve's Afghan coat on the pebbles. We huddle up for warmth, pass the bottle to and fro and decide to watch the dawn rise over Ventimiglia.

The three of us stretch out, me in the middle, on Steve's convenient coat. Soon Ulricke falls asleep. Anneliese and I talk on quietly. I pass her the Martini. Carefully she brings it to her mouth. I notice how, like many women, she drinks awkwardly from the bottle. She fits her lips around the opening and tilts head and bottle simultaneously. When you drink from the bottle like this, some of the fluid in your mouth, as you lower your head after your gulp, runs back into the bottle.

"Ow. I think I'm drunk," she says, handing it back.

I press my lips to the bottle's warm snout, try to taste her lipstick, raise the bottle, try to hold that first mouthful in my throat, swilling it around my teeth and tongue . . .

Ulricke gives a little snore, hunches herself into my left side, pressing my right side against Anneliese. Despite what you may think I want nothing more from Anneliese than what I possess now. I look out over the Mediterranean, hear the plash and rattle of the tiny sluggish waves on the pebbles, sense an ephemeral lunar grayness—a lightening—in the air.

Lunch

DATE: Monday

VENUE: Le Truc Intéressant, Lexington Street, Soho

PRESENT: Me, Gerald Vere, Melanie Swartz, Peter (Somebody) from Svenska Bank, Barry Freeman, Diane Skinner (account exec from SLL&L), Eddie Kroll (left before pudding)

MEAL: Tabbouleh chinois, roulade de foie de veau farcie, mille-feuilles de fruits d'hiver

WINE: Two Moët & Chandon nonvintage, two Sancerres, an '83 Pichon-Longueville, a big Provençal red called Mas Julienne. Port, brandy (eau de vie de prune for Diane S.).

BILL: £678 (service not included)

EXTRAS: Romeo y Julietas for Vere and Freeman; T-shirt and souvenir condiments set for Melanie; a packet of Marlboro Lights for Diane S.

COMMENTS: No piped music. Tabbouleh chinois an orthodox tabbouleh with sliced lychees mixed in. Unusual.

Roulade de foie exquisite, served on a little purée of cele-
riac. Diane S. barely touched her food, "saving up for
dessert." Mille-feuilles—8 out of 10 for the pastry. Fruits
bland. Diane S. picked up tab. Taxied me back too. Thank
you Swabold, Lang, Laing & Longmuir. Thank you very
much.

DATE: Tuesday

VENUE: Eurotel Palace, Heathrow Airport

PRESENT: Me, Diane S.

MEAL: Insalata tricolore, Dover sole, tarte aux pommes

WINE: G&T in bar, Merry Dale Chardonnay, house champagne with pud

BILL: £96 (service included)

EXTRAS: Irish coffee served in our room. £5.50 each.
20 Marlboro Lights.

COMMENTS. Almost inaudible classical Muzak. Rubbery
mozzarella. When will the British stop serving "A selection
of vegetables"? Tasteless carrots, watery broccoli, some
kind of swede. Tarte aux pommes a simple apple pie, not
flattered by translation. House champagne surprisingly
good—small bubbles, buttery, cidery. Undrunk Irish coffee—waste.

DATE: Wednesday

VENUE: Chairman's dining "set," sixth floor. Pale oak paneling. Silver. Good paintings—a small perfect Sutherland,
Alan Reynolds, two Craxtons.

PRESENT: Me, Sir Torquil, Gerald Vere, Barry Freeman, Blake Ginsberg (new CEO), some senior suit from Finance (introduced as "You know Lucy"—can't be his first name, surely? Very foreign-looking)

MEAL: Vegetable terrine, lamb chops with new potatoes, raspberries with crème fraîche. Stilton.

WINE: Hip flask in loo downstairs, then Vodkatini (could have been colder), a perfectly good Chablis, followed by a '78 Domaine de Chevalier (stunning). Port (Taylor's, missed date).

BILL: A heavy price to pay

EXTRAS: At least I saw the Sutherland.

COMMENTS: Apart from the vegetable terrine (always a total waste of time) this was superior corporate catering. Sensible. Lamb nicely pink. Superb wine. They had the grace to wait until the cheese. The condemned man had eaten a hearty meal. Fucking heartless cold fucking swine.

DATE: Thursday

VENUE: La Casa del' Luigi, Fulham Road

PRESENT: Me, Diane, (later) Jennifer

MEAL: Minestrone, spaghetti bolognese, tiramisù

WINE: G&Ts, Valpolicella, replaced by a Chianti Classico when spilled. Large grappa after Jennifer's arrival and departure.

BILL: £63 rounded up to £80. Scant gratitude.

EXTRAS: 20 Marlboro Lights. Three glasses, two plates. Dry cleaning to be notified.

COMMENTS: Minestrone was tinned, I'd swear. Alfredo's spag. bol. amazingly authentic as ever (why can't one ever achieve this at home?). He refuses to divulge his secret but I'm convinced it's the chicken livers in the ragu. Which must simmer for days, also. Watery, ancient tiramisù. Big mistake to eat so close to home. HUGE mistake. Jennifer could have walked right past. What bastard waiter called her in?

DATE: Friday

VENUE: Montrose Dining Club, Lincoln's Inn. Basement, large overlit room, long central table. Staffed by very old ex-college porters and very young monoglot girls who appear to be from Eastern Europe.

PRESENT: Me, Alisdair Lockhart

MEAL: Potted shrimps and toast, duck à l'orange, treacle tart (!)

WINE: G&Ts, club claret, club brandy

BILL: £18. (I paid. Astonishing value. Alisdair said he could add it to his bill but I insisted.)

EXTRAS: About £5000 if I know Alisdair

COMMENTS: Time travel. Back to school. This was English cuisine until quite recently; we have forgotten that this was how we all used to eat. Potted shrimps like consuming cold butter, limp toast. Duck cooked to extinction, repulsive cloying sauce. I ordered treacle tart for nostalgia's sake. (Alisdair has appalling dandruff for a comparatively young man.) I said Jennifer was being difficult, thus far. He was not sanguine. Asked if this had happened before so I told him of Jennifer's ultimatum. Spoke briefly about custody of Toby. He left early as he had to get to court. Depressing. Drank whiskey in an Irish pub.

———————————

DATE: Saturday

PLACE: My kitchen, Rostrevor Road, Fulham

PRESENT: Me and (intermittently) Birgitte, the au pair

MEAL: Raided fridge—cottage cheese and crispbread, remains of Thursday's shepherd's pie, some of Toby's little yogurt things, cheese triangles. Birgitte sent out for a pizza but I couldn't be bothered waiting.

WINE: "Three goes of gin, a lemon slice and a ten-ounce tonic . . ." Who said that? Then two glasses of Pinot Grigio, before I went down to the basement and rooted out the Ducru-Beaucaillou. Fuck it. I gave some to Birgitte, who made a face. She preferred to drink her own beer. She gave me a can when I'd finished the Beaucaillou. Strong stuff. Slept in the afternoon.

BILL: The Human Condition

EXTRAS: I miss Toby and Jennifer. I miss our usual Saturday lunch. Best lunch of the week.

COMMENTS: Music—Brahms horn trio initially but it made me want to weep. Birgitte played something rhythmic, ethnic. She gave me a tape of ocean waves breaking on a shore. "For calming," she said. Big, bighearted girl. Why would anybody eat cottage cheese? What, in terms of taste and texture, could possibly recommend it? Jennifer and her silly, perpetual diets. Perfectly slim, perfectly . . .

The cheese triangles were unbelievably tasty, ate a whole wheel's worth as I drank the Beaucaillou.

———————

DATE: Sunday. Cold, low, packed clouds, a flat, sullen light.

VENUE: Somewhere in eastern England on the 11:45 to Norwich. Writing this in the bar. On my way to Mother and Sunday lunch.

PRESENT: Me, three soldiers, a fat woman, and a thin weaselly man with a mobile phone

MEAL: Started with a Jimmyburger on the station concourse, then a couple of Scotch eggs in the bar. On the train I had a bag of salt-'n'-vinegar crisps and an egg-and-cress sandwich from the steward with the trolley. In the buffet thus far I have had a pork pie, a sausage roll, something called a "Ploughman's Bap" and a Mars bar. There is a solitary mushroom-and-salami omelette wrapped in cellophane that they will do in a microwave. Why am I still hungry?

WINE: Large vodka and orange in the station bar—vague, very temporary desire to keep my breath alcohol-free. Two cans of gin and Italian vermouth in the train before I wandered buffetward. Started drinking lager: "Speyhawk Special Strength." Notice the squaddies are drinking the same. They do quarter bottles of wine in here, I see. I've now bought a couple, having ordered the omelette. It is labeled "Red Wine." No country of origin. Tart, pungent, raw. I worry it will stain my lips. Mother will serve, as usual, Moselle and call it hock.

EXTRAS: A lot of cigarette smoke, everyone is smoking including, covertly, the steward behind the bar. Smoke seeps between the fingers of his loosely clenched fist resting on his buttocks. The fat woman is smoking. The man on the mobile phone is smoking as he mutters into his little plastic box. I have a metallic taste in my mouth, and am seized by a sudden, embittering image of Diane S.—naked, laughing.

COMMENTS: The English countryside has never looked so drained and dead under this oppressive pewter sky. The barman beckons . . . Now I have my mushroom-and-salami omelette, a piebald yellow with brown patches, steaming suspiciously, a curious, gamey but undeniably foodlike smell seems suddenly to have pervaded the entire carriage, obliterating all other odors. Everyone is looking at me. I screw the top off my "Red Wine" and fill my glass as we hurtle across Norfolk. Gastric juices squirt. I'm starving, how is this possible? My mother will have the archetype of an English Sunday lunch waiting for me. A roast, cooked gray, potatoes and two or three vegetables, a lake of gravy, cheese and biscuits, her special trifle. I look out the window at the miles of somber green. Rain is spitting on the glass and the soldiers have started to sing. Time for my omelette. I know what I am doing but it is a bad sign, this, the beginning of the end. I am deliberately setting out to ruin (because, let's face it, you cannot, before lunch, lunch) lunch.

N Is *for* N

NGUYEN N, Laotian bellelettrist and amateur philosopher. Born in Vientiane, Laos, 1883; died Paris, France, 22 February 1942. N's family was of bourgeois stock, comparatively wealthy, Francophone and Francophile. Nguyen, a precocious but somewhat unhealthy youth, yearned for Paris, but World War I delayed his arrival there until he was twenty-four.

But after humid Vientiane Paris proved noisome and frustrating. The severe winter of 1920 caused his health to fail (something cardiovascular) and he went south to recuperate, to the Côte d'Azur. Strengthened, he decided to settle there. He earned his living as a math tutor and semiprofessional table tennis player, participating in the short-lived Ping-Pong leagues that briefly flourished on that sunny littoral in the 1920s.

And it was there that he wrote his little masterpiece, *Les Analectes de Nguyen N* (Toulon: Monnier, 1928), a copy of which I found last year in Hyères, its cerise wrapper dusty and sun-bleached, its pages uncut. A sequence of epiphanic images and apothegms, its tone fragile and nervy, balancing per-ilously between the profound and the banal. "Somewhere snow is gently falling," Nguyen writes amid the mimosa and the umbrella pines, "and I still feel pain." English cannot do their tender sincerity full justice.

After the book's success Nguyen was taken up by the cul-tural salons of Paris, where he returned permanently in 1931. He is a tenant of the footnotes of literary history; the uniden-tified face at the café table; a shadowy figure on the perimeter of many a memoir and biography.

He wrote once to André Gide, who had taxed him on his unusual surname, which is not uncommon in Laos ". . . It is properly pronounced *unnnnhhhh*, effectively three syllables, the final 'h's being as plosive as possible, if you can imagine that. Ideally, after introducing me, you should be very slightly out of breath."

The war brought penury. Nguyen went to work in the kitchens of Paris's largest Vietnamese restaurant, where he discovered a talent for the decorative garnish. His lacy carrot carnations, scallion lilies and translucent turnip roses were miniature works of art. In between shifts he wrote his short autobiography, *Comment ciseler les légumes* (Paris: Plon et Noel, 1943—very rare), which was published posthumously.

Nguyen N was run over in the blackout one gloomy Feb-ruary night by a gendarme on a bicycle. He died instantly.

The Persistence
of Vision

Persistence of vision is a trick of the eye, an ability the eye possesses to fill in the gaps between discrete images and make them appear perfectly contiguous. This is what makes animation work.

Murray and Ginsberg's Dictionary of Cinema (1949)

4:05 A.M. The island. Seated on the terrace in front of my house. This is what I tried to retain. This is what I wanted to come to me unbidden from those three years. The soft explosion of a pile of leaves. A bare-breasted Gypsy girl dancing for some native soldiers. Orange snakes uncoiling in the glossy panels of an antique automobile. Big papery blue blossoms of hydrangea. A red printed smile on a square of tissue. A honeyed triangle of toast on a faience plate. Tennis in Sausalito. The huge pewtery light of the salt pans. The bleached teak decks of a motor yacht. A rare cloud trapped in a cloud-reflecting pool.

It was in the gusty autumnal pathways of the park that I first saw her. Her small dog had nosed its way into a crackling and shifting drift of plane leaves and she was tugging crossly at the lead, shouting, "Mimi, no, come on, really, you impossible beast!" in her surprisingly deep voice. But it was her wrists that held my attention first and provoked that curious breathlessness that I always associate with moments of intense irritation or intense desire. They were very thin, with the bony nodule of the wristbone, the ulna, particularly prominent as she tugged and heaved on recalcitrant Mimi's crocodile-skin leash. She was bundled up against the astringent frostiness of the day in an old ankle-length apple-green tweed coat, a black cashmere shawl and a soft felt hat that concealed her figure totally, but the length and slimness of her pale wrists and swift computations and assessments thereafter—a slightly hooked nose, sunglasses of an opaque ultramarine hue, a corkscrew of auburn hair—were enough for me to lose concentration and allow Gilbert, my adored but ineffably stupid Labrador pup, to gallop by me, unchecked, from whatever shrubbery or tree bole he was dousing, and hurl himself into Mimi's leaf-drift.

The soft explosion of dry leaves, the terrified yips and idiot barkings, the cuffs administered to Gilbert's golden rump, the apologies, the pacifying of Mimi, the crouchings-down, the straightenings-up, the removal of sunglasses, the removal of a calfskin glove from my right hand, the briefest gripping of those thin cold ringless (ringless!) fingers were achieved in a kind of roaring silence as if one half of my brain were registering the full tapestry of sounds available (the dogs, our voices and above the traffic the querulous where-the-hell-are-you? toot of an impatient motorist, blocked in by a delivery van or waiting for someone), while the other half, as if in some dust-free, shadowless laboratory, were pedantically analyzing and observing. Noting: the ability to raise one eyebrow (the left) without any change in expression; the depth of the blue hollows in the undulations of bone and skin where the clavicle joined the manubrium below her throat; the wide mouth and the perfect unevenness of her teeth. Assessing: the exact moment when to effect the introduction; the exchange of doggy arcana ("A Norfolk terrier? Quite rare, I think." "Norwich, actually." "Really?"); the casual invitation absentmindedly offered just as one was saying goodbye, about to set off: "Look, I don't suppose you'd fancy—?" The observable pause, the flick of the eye toward the east gate of the park, the decisive, independent jut of the chin and the tautening of the lips to suppress a smile as she accepted.

We sat at a small table and she rubbed a small circle, tugging her coat sleeve down over the heel of her hand, in the bleary condensation of the window to peer out at the motorcars speeding past. She chose hot chocolate and smoked a French cigarette. I had an apple juice and tried not to sneeze. Her name was—is—Golo.

Even at the wedding her father did not trouble to disguise his candid dislike for me. That he had a handsome, young, parentless, independently wealthy son-in-law whose devotion to his daughter was both profound and unequivocal seemed to make no difference at all. I asked Golo why he hated me. "Oh, Daddy's like that," she said. "He hates everybody. It's nothing to do with the fact that I'm marrying you." I asked my best friend, and best man, Max. Doctor Max thought for a while and then said: "It's obvious. He's jealous."

Of course that made it worse. We married in a small rural church stacked with the tombs and effigies of Golo's ancestors, a short canter from the family home. I had a flaming sword of indigestion rammed down my esophagus for three days preceding the ceremony which miraculously disappeared the moment I said "I do" and I knew that the old man had lost his power to frighten me anymore. I could look at his seamed, haughty face, the thinning, oiled hair and the debonair hidalgo's sideburns that he affected and feel no fear. I was not at ease, true, but I was no longer scared. "You may call me Avery now," he said, as we shook hands after the ceremony, but I never did.

At the reception the relief made me drink too much and, feeling myself unsteady, I sought a distant lavatory in which to vomit. I tickled my throat with the thin end of my tie and emptied my stomach. Patting my lips with a hand towel and feeling markedly better, I realized I had wandered into Golo's father's apartments. The bathroom was paneled in a knotty and brooding oxblood cherrywood. Many stern, blazered, cross-armed young men sitting in rows gazed proudly out from sepia photographs. Here and there among the cased memorabilia were samples of discreet erotica: breast-baring Gypsy maidens playing the tambourine for languid Zouaves; loose peignoirs slipping off shoulders at midday *levées*. And a picture of Golo, a thin and pubescent fourteen-year-old.

The room was redolent of expensive hair oils and sandalwood soaps. It was a private shrine to the sort of clubby yet perverse masculinity that I loathed—the beery sexuality of a rugby team's locker room or the officers' mess after the port has gone round. Max's observation now seemed alarmingly apt. I crumpled my face towel and threw it in the wastepaper basket. I had to get out. I opened the door.

"What the hell are you doing in here?" her father—Avery—said. He held a long cigar, ash down, in his five fingers.

"Came to say goodbye, sir." I offered my hand. "I was told you were in your sitting room."

Avery was not convinced, but, transferring his cigar, he

shook my hand all the same. "They've only just started the ball, for Christ's sake."

"Ferry to catch."

I stood in the misted blue dusk with Max, waiting for Golo, standing beside the old burnished Malvern some uncle had given us as a present, our cases strapped into the boot. Fitful orange snakes danced in the glossy bodywork from the flares burning down the drive.

"I've got to get her out of here," I said, a little hysterically. "That man is a monster. No wonder her sisters went to live with the mother."

"Stepsisters," Max said. "Golo's from the first wife."

"Oh? I didn't see her here."

"She committed suicide when Golo was five."

"Jesus. How do you know?"

"I was talking to a cousin, inside."

Max offered me a small silver box. I lifted its lid: it was full of small round unmarked pills. "My wedding present," Max said. "I rarely prescribe them. One has to have an exceptionally healthy heart, but they're guaranteed to make your honeymoon go with a zing."

We embraced and I caught a scent of the menthol jujubes Max used to suck to sweeten his breath.

"Where is that girl?" I said, my voice thick with emotion.

Max reached into the Malvern and tooted a brisk cadenza on the horn, redundantly, as Golo, dressed as far as my blurry eyes could tell in a matador's spangled suit of light, emerged through the front door and seemed to flow luminously down the stairs into my arms.

———

We honeymooned at my little house on the island. I had had its clapboard exterior repainted a lemony cream the better to offset the regulation bottle green demanded by the mayor's office. Big cloudy blue blossoms of hydrangea lined the sandy path down to the beach. Across the silver bay I could see the dark stripe of the mainland. A lone yacht slowly edged its way east. In a minute the composition would be perfect. I ached for my sketch pad.

Image. Golo sitting on the lavatory, her skirt hitched up to her thighs, her ankles footcuffed by her impossibly sheer panties. Her long pale thighs angled upward, knees meeting, her satin evening shoes just clinging to her heels as she sits on tiptoes, like a jockey straddling a thoroughbred. Except this jockey is simultaneously painting her lips vermilion without the aid of a mirror. She purses her lips, pouts and turns to offer me her best false smile.

"Mmm?"

"Perfect. I don't know how you do it."

She tears off a square of lavatory paper and prints her lips on it. Neatly folded once, it does the work it was intended for down below, before the panties are hoicked to the knee, and then Golo rises in a swoop and rustle of crêpe. There is a milli-second of buttock-cleft on view before the dressing is complete and the chrome knob is pressed and the cistern voids itself.

"Why did you quit medical school?" she asks, apropos of nothing, checking her impassive face in the mirror. Her little finger lightly touches each corner of her mouth.

"What? Because I wanted to be a painter."

"Can't you be a doctor and a painter at the same time?"

"I can't."

"What about your friend? He's a doctor and other things."

"Max? But Max is Renaissance Man. I can't compete with Max, for heaven's sake."

"Can we get a yacht?"

"Of course. But why on earth?"

"I think I want to learn to sail. Where are we going tonight?"

"The maharani's."

"How dreary."

I watched Max dicing the garlic cloves. Each clove was peeled, halved lengthways and then laid flat and held with a fingertip on the chopping board, where, with a small fine knife, the clove was sliced vertically into a fan, turned 90 degrees and sliced across again, tiny neat cubes resulting. The residue left under the finger was discarded.

"Why don't you use a press?"

"It doesn't taste the same."

We were in his garden flat in Kensington, not far from one of the hospitals where he had consulting rooms. He was cooking me supper—scallops. In oil and tomatoes. His kitchen was both efficient and picturesque. Big cleared areas for working, many pan-crowded shelves and racks and, hung here and there, hams and sausage, pimentos, chiles and garlic. Needless to say, Max was a highly accomplished cook and he liked his cuisine flavorsome.

"Thank you for my picture," he said.

"It's the view from the sitting room."

"I know." He wandered over to peer at the picture, which he had placed on a pine dresser. "You've changed the hydrangeas, or is that artistic license?"

"Well remembered. When were we there?"

"Thanks. Two summers ago. Is that the *Heliotrope*?"

"What's that?"

"The yacht I used to sail at university. You remember, you met us once at Juan-les-Pins. Something about the spinnaker. That's a nice thought. Thank you."

"It's just a yacht, I'm afraid. Isn't that enough garlic?"

He slid the garlic off the board into a pan where it spat and sizzled in the hot oil.

"How's Golo?" he said.

"Wonderful."

Later, over the cheese, he said: "Don't mind me saying this, old friend, but don't leave a woman on her own for long."

"God, I'm only away for one night. I had to see the trustees."

"I'm not talking about now. Women get bored much faster than men."

"Says who?"

"It's a well-known medical fact. Try some of this quince jelly with the cheese. Just something an old lothario told me once."

Golo is lying on her side, on the bed, naked. I stand in the doorway of the bathroom, showered, spent, happy. Propped on one elbow, she is reading a trashy Sunday paper and laughing to herself at its idiocies. At her elbow, on a faience plate I bought at Saint-Martin, is a triangle of honeyed toast. Through the window I see the sun on the bay and that obliging yacht attended by two or three seagulls. Without looking up Golo searches the bed with her right foot for the square of sunshine that was warming her flank a moment ago. She finds it and allows her foot a sunbath while she reads, reaches for her toast and bites.

"Why do you buy this rubbish? The stuff they say."

"I only get it for the funnies." I think I must be the happiest fellow in the world.

"A likely story."

We traveled that first year. I let the house in Carlyle Square to a Brazilian diplomat and we went east to India, Ceylon, Thailand. We saw out the winter with Golo's school chum Charlotte and her husband Didier Van Breuer in Sydney, Australia. Spring found us in a little house in Sausalito on another, larger bay. The exhibition of my Indian gouaches in a Broome Street gallery was a modest success. Golo developed a surprisingly effective, kicking second serve. We were never a night apart.

I felt a physical presence in my gut, like a stone lodged between my liver and my pancreas. I looked out over the dark trees of Carlyle Square and made all sorts of bargains with any number of deities.

Max came through the bedroom, running his hands through his hair, which was graying remarkably fast, I noticed, for some odd reason. He looks more tired than me, I thought.

"Relax," he said. "I'm not a gynecologist, but I would say your wife is pregnant."

I have a son. His name is Dominic. He bellows with rage, he screams, he howls. Odette, his nurse, takes him to his room. I touch Golo's face with my knuckles.

"Welcome home," I say, and from my pocket remove the ring I have had made from an emerald I bought in Bangkok. Golo slips it on her finger.

"She manages to say 'I love you,' before she dissolves in tears," I gently mock her.

She hugs me to her. "You're so sweet," she says. "And I do love you."

Didier Van Breuer to dinner at Carlyle Square. He tells us he is divorcing Charlotte. I leave the room when a messenger comes to the front door, and when I return Van Breuer is sitting hunched over his food, sobbing. It is all too terribly sad.

Summer came around again and we open up the house on the island. The new annex for Odette and Dominic blended perfectly with the rest of the house. Odette—a strong raw-boned girl, with many moles—proved to be a capable cook as well as a capable nurse. In one week we were served bouillabaisse, oursins à la provençale, marinated veal chops with ratatouille, poulet stuffed with roast garlic, pied de porc lyonnais, liver and onions. It was delicious, but too rich for me. I found myself feeling overstuffed and bilious, my throat salty and my sinal passages pungent and herby even the next morning. I fasted for twenty-four hours, drinking only distilled water, and endured a night sweat that drove Golo from the bed.

"We must smell like a tinker's camp," I said to her the day I began to feel better. "Tell Odette it's salads for the rest of the summer." By and large she complied, though from time to time a reeking stew or casserole would arrive at the table and the place would smell like a Neapolitan trattoria once again.

I found it hard to paint in the house now that its routines revolved around Dominic's noisy needs rather than my own. I was trying to complete enough work for an exhibition that a friend, who owned a little gallery in the rue Jacob, was kindly arranging for me, and so, most days I would load the panniers on my bicycle with my paints and brushes and set off for various parts of the island that were not pestered with tourists or summer residents, returning home as evening began to approach. I found a place overlooking the salt pans which promised great refulgent expanses of sky and water. I loved the salt pans with their strange poetry of dessication, though the series of watercolors I produced there, well enough done, had a lonely simplicity that seemed a little repetitive.

So it was in search of some contrasting bustle and busyness that I reluctantly ventured into one of the little ports and set up my easel by the marina. But after the serenity of the salt pans I found the presence of curious sightseers peering over my shoulder off-putting and, to be frank, my technique was found wanting when I came to render the bobbing mass of yachts and powerboats, dinghies and cruisers, that were crowded in among the piers and the jetties.

I was sitting there one midmorning, having torn up my first attempt, wondering vaguely if it would be worth looking at some Dufys that I knew hung in a provincial gallery not more than half a day's drive away, when my peripheral attention was caught by a half-glimpsed figure, male, slim in white khakis and a navy sweater, that I was convinced was familiar. You know the way your instinctive apprehension is often more sure and certain than something studied and sought for: the glance is often more accurate than the stare. I was oddly positive that I had seen someone I knew and, having nothing on the easel to detain me, I sauntered off to find out who it was.

Didier Van Breuer sat in the sunshine of the restaurant terrace with a small glass of brandy and a caffè latte on the table in front of him, shirtless with a navy blue cotton sweater. He had a small red bandanna at his throat. He looked changed since we had last seen him, older and more gaunt. He did not seem too surprised to see me (he knew I summered on the island, he said) but I was glad to discover that my instincts and my eyesight were as sharp and shrewd as they had always been. He was cordial, with none of that reserve I had always associated with him.

"Where are you staying?" I asked.

He pointed to the harbor, at a vast gin-palace of a motor yacht with a single tall funnel (yellow with a magenta stripe). Crew members swabbed down bleached teak decks; brown water was being pumped from bilges. He was alone, he told me, on an endless meandering summer cruise trying to forget Charlotte and her grotesque betrayal (she was living with Didier's estranged son). I asked him to dinner that night (I had seen Odette empty almost an entire tin of cumin into a lobster stew) but he declined, saying they were setting sail for the Azores later. He finished his drink and we wandered around the quay to his boat (his trousers were pale blue, I noticed with a private smile; however vigilant, the corner of your eye cannot achieve 20/20 vision). He had changed the name from *Charlotte III* to *Clymene*, who, he told me, with harsh irony, was the mistress of the sun. He invited me on board and we strolled through the empty staterooms smoking cigars, the warm buttock of a brandy goblet cupped in my tight palm. I felt sad for him, with his pointless wealth and the cheerless luxury of his life, and felt sad myself as the boat reminded me of Pappi's old schooner, the *Vergissmeinnicht*, and my lost childhood. He had a rather fine Dufy in the dining room and I took the opportunity to make a few quick notes and sketches while he went upstairs to make a telephone call.

Nota bene. To be remembered: the serene roseate beauty of the summer dusk as I cycled homeward, a little drunk, a rare cloud trapped in a cloud-reflecting puddle at the side of the road. To be remembered: my almost insupportable feeling of happiness.

4 a.m. I am alone on the terrace of my small house, looking east beyond my blue hydrangeas toward the mainland, wait-

ing for the sun to rise. I wonder how many people there are on that mainland as miserable as I am.

Golo's note was terse. She had left me and our child. She was no longer in love with me. There was another man in her life whose identity she would not reveal at this moment. I must not look for her. She would be in touch with me in due course. This was the only way. She needed none of my money. She asked my forgiveness and understanding and hoped, for the sake of Dominic, that we could remain friends.

Odette said simply that during the day Madame had received and made numerous phone calls, had packed one suitcase and then, at about four o'clock, she heard the taxi claxoning for her in the lane. She was going to visit her family, she had told Odette, she had left a note for me and was gone.

I wasted no time. I drove at once back to the port, where of course there was no sign of the *Clymene*. En route for the Azores or God knew where. I returned to my house (not *our* house anymore) and cried a few hot tears of rage and frustration over my son's cot (*my* son, not *our* son anymore) until I woke him and he began to bawl as well. I drank half a bottle of Pernod, then drove the car to the ferry and was transported to the mainland. I spent a fruitless hour searching for a "Venus of the Crossroads," as Pappi used to refer to them, feeling the urge for revenge slowly ebb from me. At around midnight, in an overlit dockside bar I halfheartedly bought a large woman with bobbed hair and a tight jersey a few drinks but then lost my nerve. On the last ferry back to the island a bearded youngster played some form of Hawaiian music on a guitar.

The sky is lightening, a pale cornflower blue shading into lemon; my dead eyes watch the beautiful transformation, unmarveling. I must think, I must clarify my thoughts. The betrayed husband is always the last to know, they say. Didier Van Breuer. Were our friends in Sydney, Australia, all laughing behind my back that winter? What had made Didier come to our house to announce his separation? What had made him break down that way over the meal? What had been said while I was out of the room? To end this stream of answerless questions I force myself to think of Encarnación, a Mexican girl I had briefly loved and to whom I had once thought of proposing. Dear, lissome Encarna, some kind of ex-athlete, a hurdler or swimmer. So different from Golo. I think of a meal we shared in New York, that little restaurant in New York, south of Greenwich Village, where she cajoled me into eating a pungent, shouting salsa from her native province that made my eyes water, obliging me to suck peppermints for days . . .

This is what I must retain. These are the fragments I must hoard from these last three years. The soft explosion of a pile of leaves. The querulous where-the-hell-are-you? tooting of a waiting motorist. The scent of menthol jujubes. A lone yacht on a silver bay. The immaculate dicing of a garlic clove. The dark trees of Carlyle Square. Oursins à la provençale. A slim male figure in white khakis and a navy sweater. A tin of cumin. A taxi claxoning in the lane. A pungent, shouting salsa that obliged me to suck peppermints for days.

Cork

O homem não é um animal
É uma carne inteligente
Embora às vezes doente.

(A man is not an animal;
Is intelligent flesh,
Although sometimes ill.)

Fernando Pessoa

MY NAME IS Lily Campendonc. A long time ago I used to live in Lisbon.

I lived in Lisbon between 1929 and 1935. A beautiful city, but melancholy.

Boscán, Christmas 1934: "We never love anyone. Not really. We only love our idea of another person. It is some conception of our own that we love. We love ourselves, in fact."

"Mrs. Campendonc?"
   "Yes?"

"May I be permitted to have a discreet word with you? Discreetly?"

"Of course."

He did not want this word to take place in the office, so we left the building and walked down the rua Serpa toward the Arsenal. It was dark, we had been working late, but the night was warm.

"Here, please. I think this small café will suit."

I agreed. We entered and sat at a small table in the rear. I asked for a coffee and he for a small glass of *vinho verde*. Then he decided to collect the order himself and went to the bar to do so. While he was there I noticed him drink a brandy standing at the bar, quickly, in one swift gulp.

He brought the drinks and sat down.

"Mrs. Campendonc, I'm afraid I have some bad news." His thin taut features remained impassive. Needlessly he re-straightened his straight bow tie.

"And what would that be?" I resolved to be equally calm.

He cleared his throat, looked up at the mottled ceiling and smiled vaguely.

"I am obliged to resign," he said. "I hereby offer you one month's notice."

I tried to keep the surprise off my face. I frowned. "That *is* bad news, Senhor Boscán."

"I am afraid I had no choice."

"May I ask why?"

"Of course, of course, you have every right." He thought for a while, saying nothing, printing neat circles of condensation on the tan scrubbed wood of the table with the bottom of his wineglass.

"The reason is . . ." he began, "and if you will forgive me I will be entirely candid—the reason is," and at this he looked me in the eye, "that I am very much in love with you, Mrs. Campendonc."

The material of which this monograph treats has become of double interest because of its shrouded mystery, which has never been pierced to the extent of giving the world a complete and comprehensive story. The mysticism is not associated with its utility and general uses, as these are well known, but rather with its chemical makeup, composition and its fascinating and extraordinary character.

Consul Schenk's Report
on the Manufacture of Cork (Leipzig, 1890)

After my husband, John Campendonc, died in 1932, I decided to stay on in Lisbon. I knew enough about the business, I told myself, and in any event could not bear the thought of returning to England and his family. In his will he left the company—the Campendonc Cork Company Ltd.—to me with instructions that it should continue as a going concern under the family name or else be sold. I made my decision and reassured those members of John's family who tried earnestly to dissuade me that I knew exactly what I was doing, and besides, there was Senhor Boscán who would always be there to help.

I should tell you a little about John Campendonc first, I suppose, before I go on to Boscán.

John Campendonc was twelve years older than me, a small strong Englishman, very fair in coloring, with fine blond hair that was receding from his forehead. His body was well muscled with a tendency to run to fat. I was attracted to him on our first meeting. He was not handsome—his features were oddly lopsided—but there was a vigor about him that was contagious, and that characterized his every movement and preoccupation. He read vigorously, for example, leaning forward over his book or newspaper, frowning, turning and smoothing down the pages with a flick and crack and a brisk stroke of his palm. He walked everywhere at high speed and his habitual pose was to thrust his left hand in the pocket of his coat—thrust strongly down—and, with his right hand, to smooth his hair back in a series of rapid caresses. Consequently his coats were always distorted on the left, the pocket bulged and baggy, sometimes torn, the constant strain on the seams inevitably proving too great. In this manner he wore out three or four suits a year. Shortly before he died I found a tailor in the rua Garrett who would make him a suit with three identical coats. So for John's fortieth birthday I presented him with an assortment of suits—flannel, tweed and cotton drill—consisting of three pairs of trousers and nine coats. He was very amused.

I retain a strong and moving image of him. It was about two weeks before his death and we had gone down to Cascais for a picnic and a bathe in the sea. It was late afternoon and the beach was deserted. John stripped off his clothes and ran naked into the sea, diving easily through the breakers. I could not—and still cannot—swim and so sat on the running board of our motorcar, smoked a cigarette and watched him splash about in the waves. Eventually he emerged and strode up the beach toward me, flicking water from his hands.

"Freezing," he shouted from some ways off. "Freezing freezing freezing!"

This is how I remember him, confident, ruddy and noisy in his nakedness. The wide slab of his chest, his fair, open face, his thick legs darkened with slick wet hair, his balls clenched and shrunken with cold, his penis a tense white stub. I laughed at him and pointed at his groin. Such a tiny thing, I said, laughing. He stood there, hands on his hips, trying to look offended. Big enough for you, Lily Campendonc, he said, grinning, you wait and see.

Two weeks and two days later his heart failed him and he was dead and gone forever.

Why do I tell you so much about John Campendonc? It will help explain Boscán, I think.

The cork tree has in no wise escaped from disease and infections; on the contrary it has its full allotted share, which worries the growers more than the acquiring of a perfect texture. Unless great care is taken, all manner of ailments can corrupt and weaken fine cork and prevent this remarkable material from attaining its full potential.

Consul Schenk's Report

Agostinho da Silva Boscán kissed me one week after he had resigned. He worked out his month's notice scrupulously and dutifully. Every evening he came to my office to report on the day's business and present me with letters and contracts to sign. On this particular evening, I recall, we were going over a letter of complaint to a cork grower in Elvas—hitherto reliable—whose cork planks proved to be riddled with ant borings. Boscán was standing beside my chair, his right hand flat on the leather top of the desk, his forefinger slid beneath the upper page of the letter, ready to turn it over. Slowly and steadily he translated the Portuguese into his impeccable English. It was hot and I was a little tired. I found I was not concentrating on the sonorous monotone of his voice. My gaze left the page of the letter and focused on his hand, flat on the desktop. I saw its even, pale brownness, like milky coffee, the dark glossy hairs that grew beneath the knuckles and the first joint of the fingers, the nacreous shine of his fingernails . . . the pithy edge of his white cuffs, beginning to fray . . . I could smell a faint musky perfume coming off him—farinaceous and sweet—from the lotion he put on his hair, and mingled with that his own scent, sour and salt . . . His suit was too heavy, his only suit, a worn shiny blue serge, made in Madrid, he told me, too hot for a summer night in Lisbon . . . Quietly, I inhaled and my nostrils filled with the smell of Agostinho Boscán.

"If you say you love me, Senhor Boscán," I interrupted him, "why don't you do something about it?"

"I am," he said after a pause. "I'm leaving."

He straightened. I did not turn, keeping my eyes on the letter.

"Isn't that a bit cowardly?"

"Well," he said. "It's true. I would like to be a bit less . . . cowardly. But there is a problem. Rather a serious problem."

Now I turned. "What's that?"

"I think I'm going mad."

My name is Lily Campendonc, née Jordan. I was born in Cairo in 1908. In 1914 my family moved to London. I was educated there and in Paris and Geneva. I married John Campendonc in 1929 and we moved to Lisbon, where he ran the family's cork processing factory. He died of a coronary attack in October 1931. I had been a widow for nine months before I kissed another man, my late husband's office manager. I was twenty-four years old when I spent my first Christmas with Agostinho da Silva Boscán.

The invitation came, typewritten on a lined sheet of cheap writing paper.

My dear Lily,

I invite you to spend Christmas with me. For three days—24, 25, 26 December—I will be residing in the village of Manjedoura. Take the train to Cintra and then a taxi from the station. My house is at the east end of the village, painted white with green shutters. It would make me very happy if you could come, even for a day. There are only two conditions. One, you must address me only as Balthazar Cabral. Two, please do not depilate yourself—anywhere.

Your good friend,
Agostinho Boscán

"Balthazar Cabral" stood naked beside the bed I was lying in. His penis hung long and thin, but slowly fattening, shifting. Uncircumcised. I watched him pour a little olive oil into the palm of his hand and grip himself gently. He pulled at his penis, smearing it with oil, watching it grow erect under his touch. Then he pulled the sheet off me and sat down. He wet his fingers with the oil again and reached to feel me.

"What's happening?" I could barely sense his moving fingers.

"It's an old trick," he said. "Roman centurions discovered it in Egypt." He grinned. "Or so they say."

I felt oil running off my inner thighs onto the bedclothes. Boscán clambered over me and spread my legs. He was thin and wiry, his flat chest shadowed with fine hairs, his nipples were almost black. The beard he had grown made him look strangely younger.

He knelt in front of me. He closed his eyes.

"Say my name, Lily, say my name."

I said it. Balthazar Cabral. Balthazar Cabral. Balthazar Cabral . . .

After the first stripping the cork tree is left in the juvenescent state to regenerate. Great care must be taken in the stripping not to injure the inner skin or epidermis at any stage in the process, for the life of the tree depends on its proper preservation. If it is injured at any point, growth there ceases and the spot remains forever afterward scarred and uncovered.

Consul Schenk's Report

I decided not to leave the house that first day. I spent most of the time in bed, reading or sleeping. Balthazar brought me food—small cakes and coffee. In the afternoon he went out for several hours. The house we were in was square and simple and set in a tangled uncultivated garden. The ground floor consisted of a sitting room and a kitchen, and above that were three bedrooms. There was no lavatory or bathroom. We used chamber pots to relieve ourselves. We did not wash.

Balthazar returned in the early evening, bringing with him some clothes that he asked me to put on. There was a small short cerise jacket with epaulets but no lapels—it looked vaguely German or Swiss—a simple white shirt and some black cotton trousers with a drawstring at the waist. The jacket was small, even for me, tight across my shoulders, the sleeves short at my wrists. I wondered if it belonged to a boy.

I dressed in the clothes he had brought and stood before him as he looked at me intently, concentrating. After a while he asked me to pin my hair up.

"Whose jacket is this?" I asked as I did so.

"Mine," he said.

We sat down to dinner. Balthazar had cooked the food. Tough stringy lamb in an oily gravy. A plate of beans the color of pistachio. Chunks of grayish spongy bread torn from a flat crusty loaf.

On Christmas Day we went out and walked for several miles along unpaved country roads. It was a cool morning with a fresh breeze. On our way back home we were caught in a shower of rain and took shelter under an olive tree, waiting for it to pass. I sat with my back against the trunk and smoked a cigarette. Balthazar sat cross-legged on the ground and scratched designs in the earth with a twig. He wore heavy boots and coarse woolen trousers. His new beard was un-even—dense around his mouth and throat, skimpy on his cheeks. His hair was uncombed and greasy. The smell of the rain falling on the dry earth was strong—sour and ferrous, like old cellars.

That night we lay side by side in bed, hot and exhausted. I slipped my hands in the creases beneath my breasts and drew them out, my fingers moist and slick. I scratched my neck. I could smell the sweat on my body. I turned. Balthazar was sitting up, one knee raised, the sheet flung off him, his shoulders against the wooden headboard. On his side of the bed was an oil lamp set on a stool. A small brown moth fluttered crazily around it, its big shadow bumping on the ceiling. I felt a sudden huge contentment spill through me. My bladder was full and was aching slightly, but with the happiness came a profound lethargy that made the effort required to reach below the bed for the enamel chamber pot prodigious.

I reached out and touched Balthazar's thigh.

"You can go tomorrow," he said. "If you want."

"No, I'll stay on," I said instantly, without thinking. "I'm enjoying myself. I'm glad I'm here." I hauled myself up to sit beside him.

"I want to see you in Lisbon," I said, taking his hand.

"No, I'm afraid not."

"Why?"

"Because after tomorrow you will never see Balthazar Cabral again."

From this meager description we now at least have some idea of what "corkwood" is and have some indication of the constant care necessary to ensure a successful gathering or harvest, while admitting that the narration in no wise does justice to this most interesting material. We shall now turn to examine it more closely and see what it really is, how this particular formation comes about and its peculiarities.

Consul Schenk's Report

Boscán: "One of my problems, one of my mental problems, rather—and how can I convince you of its effect?—horrible, horrible beyond words—is my deep and abiding fear of insanity . . . Of course it goes without saying; such a deep fear of insanity is insanity itself."

I saw nothing of Boscán for a full year. Having left my employ, he then, I believe, became a freelance translator, working for any firm that would give him a job and not necessarily in the cork industry. Then came Christmas 1933 and another invitation arrived, written on a thick buff card with deckle edges in a precise italic hand, in violet ink:

> Senhora Campendonc, do me the honor of spending the festive season in my company. I shall be staying at the Avenida Palace hotel, rooms 35–38, from 22 to 26 December inclusive.
>
> Your devoted admirer,
J. Melchior Vasconcelles
>
> P.S. Bring many expensive clothes and scents. I have jewels.

Boscán's suite in the Avenida Palace was on the fourth floor. The bellhop referred to me as Senhora Vasconcelles. Boscán greeted me in the small vestibule and made the bellhop leave my cases there.

Boscán was dressed in a pale gray suit. His face was thinner, clean-shaven and his hair was sleek, plastered down on his head with macassar. In his shiny hair I could see the stiff furrows made from the teeth of the comb.

When the bellhop had gone we kissed. I could taste the mint from his mouthwash on his lips.

Boscán opened a small leather suitcase. It was full of jewels, paste jewels, rhinestones, strings of artificial pearls, diamante brooches and marcasite baubles. This was his plan, he said: this Christmas our gift to each other would be a day. I would dedicate a day to him, and he one to me.

"Today you must do everything I tell you," he said. "Tomorrow is yours."

"All right," I said. "But I won't do everything you tell me to, I warn you."

"Don't worry, Lily, I will ask nothing indelicate of you."

"Agreed. What shall I do?"

"All I want you to do is to wear these jewels."

The suite was large: a bathroom, two bedrooms and a capacious sitting room. Boscán/Vasconcelles kept the curtains drawn, day and night. In one corner was a freestanding cast-iron stove that one fed from a wooden box full of coal. It was warm and dark in the suite; we were closed off from the noise of the city; we could have been anywhere.

We did nothing. Absolutely nothing. I wore as many of his cheap trinkets as my neck, blouse, wrists and fingers could carry. We ordered food and wine from the hotel kitchen, which was brought up at regular intervals, Vasconcelles himself collecting everything in the vestibule. I sat and read in the electric gloom, my jewels winking and flashing merrily at the slightest shift of position. Vasconcelles smoked short stubby cigars and offered me fragrant oval cigarettes. The hours crawled by. We smoked, we ate, we drank. For want of anything better to do I consumed most of a bottle of champagne and dozed off. I awoke, fuzzy and irritated, to find Vasconcelles had drawn a chair up to the sofa I was slumped on and was sitting there, elbows on knees, chin on fists, staring at me. He asked me questions about the business, what I had been doing in the last year, had I enjoyed my trip home to England, had the supply of cork from Elvas improved and so on. He was loquacious, we talked a great deal, but I could think of nothing to ask him in return. J. Melchior Vasconcelles was, after all, a complete stranger to me, and I sensed it would put his tender personality under too much strain to inquire about his

circumstances and the fantastical life he led. All the same, I
was very curious, knowing Boscán as I did.

"This suite must be very expensive," I said.

"Oh yes. But I can afford it. I have a car outside too. And a
driver. We could go for a drive."

"If you like."

"It's an American car. A Packard."

"Wonderful."

That night, when we made love in the fetid bedroom he
asked me to keep my jewels on.

"It's your day today."

"Thank you. Merry Christmas."

"And the same to you . . . What do you want me to do?"

"Take all your clothes off."

I made Vasconcelles remain naked for the entire day. It was
at first amusing and then intriguing to watch his mood
slowly change. Initially he was excited, sexually, and regularly
aroused. But then, little by little, he became self-conscious
and awkward. At one stage in the day I watched him filling the
stove with coal, one-handed, the other hand cupped reflex-
ively around his genitals, like adolescent boys I had once seen
jumping into the sea off a breakwater at Cidadela. Later still,
he grew irritable and restless, pacing up and down, not content to sit and talk out the hours as we had done the day
before.

In midafternoon I put on a coat and went out for a drive,
leaving him behind in the suite. The big Packard was there, as
he had said, and a driver. I had him drive me down to Estoril
and back. I was gone for almost three hours.

When I returned Vasconcelles was asleep, lying on top of

the bed in the hot bedroom. He was deeply asleep, his mouth open, his arms and legs spread. His chest rose and fell slowly and I saw how very thin he was, his skin stretched tight over his ribs. When I looked closely I could see the shiver and bump of his palpitating heart.

Before dinner he asked me if he could put on his clothes. When I refused his request it seemed to make him angry. I reminded him of our gifts and their rules. But to compensate him I wore a tight sequined gown, placed his flashy rings on my fingers and roped imitation pearls around my neck. My wrists tickled and clattered with preposterous rhinestone bangles. So we sat and ate: me, Lily Campendonc, splendid in my luminous jewels and, across the table, J. Melchior Vasconcelles, surly and morose, picking at his Christmas dinner, a crisp linen napkin spread modestly across his thighs.

The various applications of cork that we are now going to consider are worthy of description, as each application has its *raison d'être* in one or more of the physical or chemical properties of this marvelous material. Cork possesses three key properties that are unique in a natural substance. They are: impermeability, elasticity and lightness.

Consul Schenk's Report

I missed Boscán after this second Christmas with him, much more—strangely—than I had after the first. I was very busy in the factory that year—1934—as we were installing machinery to manufacture Kamptulicon, a soft, unresounding cork carpet made from cork powder and india rubber and much favored by hospitals and the reading rooms of libraries. My new manager—a dour, reasonably efficient fellow called Pimentel—saw capably to most of the problems that arose but refused to accept any responsibility for all but the most minor decisions. As a result I was required to be present whenever anything of significance had to be decided, as if I functioned as a symbol of delegatory power, a kind of managerial chaperone. I thought of Boscán often, and many nights I wanted to be with him. On those occasions, as I lay in bed dreaming of Christmases past and, I hoped, Christmases to come, I thought I would do anything he asked of me—or so I told myself.

One evening at the end of April I was leaving a shop on the rua Conceição, where I had been buying a christening present for my sister's second child, when I saw Boscán enter a café, the Trinidade. I walked slowly past the door and looked inside. It was cramped and gloomy and there were no women clients. In my glimpse I saw Boscán leaning eagerly across a table, around which sat half a dozen men, showing them a photograph; at first they peered at it, frowning, and then they broke into wide smiles. I walked on, agitated, this moment frozen in my mind's eye. It was the first time I had seen Boscán, and Boscán's life, separate from myself. I felt unsettled and oddly envious. Who were these men? Friends or colleagues? I wanted suddenly and absurdly to share in that moment of the offered photograph, to frown and then grin conspiratorially like the others.

I waited outside the Trinidade sitting in the back of my motorcar with the windows open and the blinds down. I made Julião, my old chauffeur, take off his peaked cap. Boscán eventually emerged at about 7:45 and walked briskly to the tramway center at the Rocio. He climbed aboard a No. 2, which we duly followed until he stepped down from it near São Vicente. He set off down the steep alleyways into the Mouraria. Julião and I left the car and followed him discreetly down a series of *boqueirão*—dim and noisome streets that led down to the Tagus. Occasionally there would be a sharp bend and we would catch a glimpse of the wide sprawling river shining below in the moonlight and beyond the scatter of lights from Almada on the southern bank.

Boscán entered through the door of a small decrepit house. The steps up to the threshold were worn and concave, the tiles above the porch were cracked and slipping. A blurry yellow light shone from behind drab lace curtains. Julião stopped a passerby and asked who lived there. Senhor Boscán, he was told, with his mother and three sisters.

"Mrs. Campendonc!"

"Mr. Boscán." I sat down opposite him. When the surprise and shock began to leave his face, I saw that he looked pale and tired. His fingers touched his bow tie, his lips, his earlobes. He was smoking a small cigar, chocolate brown, and wearing his old blue suit.

"Mrs. Campendonc, this is not really a suitable establishment for a lady."

"I wanted to see you." I touched his hand, but he jerked it away, as if my fingers burned him.

"It's impossible. I'm expecting some friends."

"Are you well? You look tired. I miss you."

His gaze flickered around the café. "How is the Kamptulicon going? Pimentel is a good man."

"Come to my house. This weekend."

"Mrs. Campendonc . . ." His tone was despairing.

"Call me Lily."

He steepled his fingers. "I'm a busy man. I live with my mother and three sisters. They expect me home in the evening."

"Take a holiday. Say you're going to . . . to Spain for a few days."

"I only take one holiday a year."

"Christmas."

"They go to my aunt in Coimbra. I stay behind to look after the house."

A young man approached the table. He wore a ludicrous yellow overcoat that reached down to his ankles. He was astonished to see me sitting there. Boscán looked even more ill as he introduced us. I have forgotten his name.

I said goodbye and went toward the door. Boscán caught up with me.

"At Christmas," he said quietly. "I'll see you at Christmas."

A postcard. A sepia view of the Palace of Queen Maria Pia, Cintra:

> I will be one kilometer west of the main beach at Paço de Arcos. I have rented a room in the Casa de Bizoma. Please arrive at dawn on 25 December and depart at sunset.
>
> I am your friend,
Gaspar Barbosa

The bark of the cork tree is removed every eight to ten years, the quality of the cork improving with each successive stripping. Once the section of cork is removed from the tree the outer surface is scraped and cleaned. The sections—wide curved planks—are flattened by heating them over a fire and submitting them to pressure on a flat surface. In the heating operation the surface is charred, and thereby the pores are closed up. It is this process that the industry terms the "nerve" of cork. This is cork at its most valuable. A cork possesses "nerve" when its significant properties—lightness, impermeability, elasticity—are sealed in the material forever.

Consul Schenk's Report

In the serene, urinous light of dawn the beach at Paço de Arcos looked slate gray. The seaside cafés were closed up and summoned up impressions of dejection and decrepitude as only out-of-season holiday resorts can. To add to this melancholy scene a fine cold rain blew off the Atlantic. I stood beneath my umbrella on the coast road and looked about me. To the left I could just make out the tower of Belém. To the right the hills of Cintra were shrouded in a heavy opaque mist. I turned and walked up the road toward the Casa de Bizoma. As I drew near I could see Boscán sitting on a balcony on the second floor. All other windows on this side of the hotel were firmly shuttered.

A young girl, of about sixteen years, let me in and led me up to his room.

Boscán was wearing a monocle. On a table behind him were two bottles of brandy. We kissed, we broke apart.

"Lise," he said. "I want to call you Lise."

Even then, even that day, I said no. "That's the whole point," I reminded him. "I'm me—Lily—whoever you are."

He inclined his body forward in a mock bow. "Gaspar Barbosa . . . Would you like something to drink?"

I drank some brandy and then allowed Barbosa to undress me, which he did with pedantic diligence and great delicacy. When I was naked he knelt before me and pressed his lips against my groin, burying his nose in my pubic hair. He hugged me, still kneeling, his arms strong around the backs of my thighs, his head turned sideways in my lap. When he began to cry softly, I raised him up and led him over to the narrow bed. He undressed and we climbed in, huddling up together, our legs interlocking. I reached down to touch him.

"I don't know what's wrong," he said. "I don't know."

"We'll wait."

"Don't forget you have to go at sunset. Remember."

"I won't."

We made love later, but it was not very satisfactory. He seemed listless and tired—nothing like Balthazar Cabral and Melchior Vasconcelles.

At noon, the hotel restaurant was closed, so we ate a simple lunch he had brought himself: some bread, some olives, some tart sheep's-milk cheese, some oranges and almonds. By then he was on to the second bottle of brandy. After lunch I smoked a cigarette. I offered him one—I had noticed he had not smoked all day—which he accepted but which he extinguished after a couple of puffs.

"I have developed a mysterious distaste for tobacco," he said, pouring himself some more brandy.

In the afternoon we tried to make love again but failed.

"It's my fault," he said. "I'm not well."

I asked him why I had had to arrive at dawn and why I had to leave at sunset. He told me it was because of a poem he had written, called "The Roses of the Gardens of the God Adonis."

"You wrote? Boscán?"

"No, no. Boscán has only written one book of poems, years ago. These are mine, Gaspar Barbosa's."

"What's it about?" The light was going; it was time for me to leave.

"Oh . . ." He thought. "Living and dying."

He quoted me the line that explained the truncated nature of my third Christmas with Agostinho Boscán. He sat at the table before the window, wearing a dirty white shirt and the trousers of his blue serge suit, and poured himself a tumblerful of brandy.

"It goes like this—roughly. I'm translating: 'Let us make our lives last one day,'" he said. "'So there is night before and night after the little that we last.'"

The uses to which corkwood may be put are unlimited. And yet when we speak of uses it is only those that have developed by reason of the corkwood's own peculiarity and not the great number it has been adapted to, for perhaps its utility will have no end and, in my estimation, its particular qualities are little appreciated. At any rate it is the most wonderful bark of its kind, its service has been a long one and its benefits, even as a stopper, have been many. A wonderful material truly, and of interest so full that it seems I have failed to do it justice in my humble endeavor to describe the *Quercus suber* of Linnaeus— cork.

Consul Schenk's Report

Boscán, during, I think, that last Christmas: "You see, because I am nothing, I can imagine *anything*. . . If I were something, I would be unable to imagine."

It was in early December 1936 that I received my last communication from Agostinho Boscán. I was waiting to hear from him, as I had received an offer for the company from the Armstrong Cork Company and was contemplating a sale and, possibly, a return to England.

I was in my office one morning when Pimentel knocked on the door and said there was a Senhora Boscán to see me. For an absurd, exquisite moment I thought this might prove to be Agostinho's most singular disguise, but remembered he had three sisters and a mother still living. I knew before she was shown in that she came with news of Boscán's death.

Senhora Boscán was small and tubby with a meek pale face. She wore black and fiddled constantly with the handle of her umbrella as she spoke. Her brother had requested specifically that I be informed of his death when it arrived. He had passed away two nights ago.

"What did he die of?"

"Cirrhosis of the liver . . . He was . . . My brother had become an increasingly heavy drinker. He was very un-happy."

"Was there anything else for me, that he said? Any message?"

Senhora Boscán cleared her throat and blinked. "There is no message."

"I'm sorry?"

"That is what he asked me to say: 'There is no message.'"

"Ah." I managed to disguise my smile by offering Senhora Boscán a cup of coffee. She accepted. "We will all miss him," she said. "Such a good quiet man."

From an obituary of Agostinho da Silva Boscán:

. . . Boscán was born in 1888 in Durban, South Africa, where his father was Portuguese consul. He was the youngest of four children, the three elder being sisters. It was in South Africa that he received a British education and where he learned to speak English. Boscán's father died when he was seventeen, and the family returned to Lisbon, where Boscán was to reside for the rest of his life. He worked primarily as a commercial translator and office manager for various industrial concerns, but mainly in the cork business. In 1916 he published a small collection of poems, *Insensivel*, written in English. The one Portuguese critic who noticed them, and who wrote a short review, described them as "a sad waste." Boscán was active for a while in Lisbon literary circles and would occasionally publish poems, translations and articles in the magazine *Sombra*. The death of his closest friend, Xavier Quevedo, who committed suicide in Paris in 1924, provoked a marked and sudden change in his personality, which became increasingly melancholic and irrational from then on. He never married. His life can only be described as uneventful.

Loose Continuity

I AM STANDING on the corner of Westwood and Wilshire, just down from the Mobil gas station, waiting. There is a coolish breeze just managing to blow from somewhere, and I am glad of it. Nine o'clock in the morning and it's going to be another hot one, for sure. For the third or fourth time I needlessly go over and inspect the concrete foundation, noting again that the power lines have been properly installed and that the extra bolts I have requested are duly there. Where is everybody? I look at my watch, light another cigarette and begin to grow vaguely worried: have I picked the wrong day? Has my accent confused Mr. Koenig (he is always asking me to repeat myself)? . . .

A bright curtain—blues and ochres—boils and billows from an apartment window across the street. It sets a forgotten corner of my mind working—who had drapes like that, once? Who owned a skirt that was similar, or perhaps a tie?

A claxon honks down Wilshire and I look up to see Spencer driving the crane, pulling slowly across two lanes of traffic and coming to a halt at the curb.

He swings down from the cab and takes off his cap. His hair is getting longer, losing that army crop.

"Sorry I'm late, Miss Velk, the depot was, you know, crazy, impossible."

"Doesn't matter, it's not here anyway."

"Yeah, right." Spencer moves over and crouches down at the concrete plinth, checking the power-line connection, touching and jiggling the bolts and their brackets. He goes around the back of the crane and sets out the wooden MEN AT WORK signs, then reaches into his pocket and hands me a crumpled sheet of flimsy.

"The permit," he explains. "We got till noon."

"Even on a Sunday?"

"Even on a Sunday. Even in Los Angeles." He shrugs. "Even in 1945. Don't worry, Miss Velk. We got plenty of time."

I turn away, a little exasperated. "As long as it gets here," I say with futile determination, as if I had the power to threaten. The drape streams out of the window suddenly, like a banner, and catches the sun. Then I remember: like the wall hanging Utta had done. The one that Tobias bought.

Spencer asks me if he should go phone the factory but I say give them an extra half hour. I am remembering another Sunday morning, sunny like this one but not as hot, and half the world away, and I can see myself walking up Grillparzerstrasse, taking the shortcut from the station, my suitcase heavy in my hand, and hoping, wondering, now that I have managed to catch the dawn train from Sorau, if Tobias will be able to find some time to see me alone that afternoon . . .

Gudrun Velk walked slowly up Grillparzerstrasse, enjoying the sun, her body canted over to counterbalance the weight of her suitcase. She was wearing . . . (What was I wearing?) She was wearing baggy cotton trousers with the elasticated cuffs at the ankles, a sky blue blouse and an embroidered felt jacket with a motif of jousters and strutting chargers. Her fair hair was down and she wore no makeup; she was thinking about Tobias, and whether they might see each other that day, and whether they might make love. Thinking about Utta, if she would be up by now. Thinking about the two thick skeins of still-damp blue wool in her suitcase, wool that she had dyed herself late the night before at the mill in Sorau and that she felt sure would finish her rug perfectly and, most importantly, in a manner that would please Paul.

Paul came to the weaving workshop often. Small, with dull olive skin and large eyes below a high forehead, eyes seemingly brimming with unshed tears. He quietly moved from loom to loom and the weavers would slip out of their seats to let him have an unobstructed view. Gudrun had started her big knotted rug, and he stood in front of it for some minutes, silently contemplating the first squares and circles. She waited; sometimes he looked, said nothing and moved on. Now, though, he said: "I like the shapes but the yellow is wrong, it needs more lemon, especially set beside that peach color." He shrugged, adding, "In my opinion." That was when she started to go to his classes on color theory and unpicked the work she had done and began again. She told him: "I'm weaving my rug based on your chromatic principles." He was pleased, she thought. He said politely that in that case he would follow its progress with particular interest.

He was not happy at the Institute, she knew; since Meyer had taken over the mood had changed, was turning against Paul and the other painters. Meyer was against them, she had been told, he felt they smacked of Weimar, the bad old days. Tobias was the same: "Bogus-advertising-theatricalism," he would state. "We should've left all that behind." What the painters did was "decorative," need one say more? So Paul was gratified to find someone who responded to his theories instead of mocking them, and in any case the mood in the weaving workshops was different, what with all the young women. There was a joke in the Institute that the women revered him, called him "the dear Lord." He did enjoy the time he spent there, he told Gudrun later, of all the workshops it was the weavers he would miss most, he said, if the day came for him to leave—all the girls, all the bright young women.

Spencer leans against the pole that holds the power lines. The sleeve of his check shirt falls back to reveal more of his burned arm. It looks pink and new and oddly, finely ridged, like bark or like the skin you get on hot milk as it cools. He taps a rhythm on the creosoted pole with his thumb and the two remaining fingers on his left hand. I know the burn goes the length of his arm and then some more, but the hand has taken the full brunt. He turns and sees me staring.

"How's the arm?" I say.

"I've got another graft next week. We're getting there, slow but sure."

"What about this heat? Does it make it worse?"

"It doesn't help, but . . . I'd rather be here than Okinawa," he says. "Damn right."

"Of course," I say, "of course."

"Yeah." He exhales and seems on the point of saying something—he is talking more about the war, these days, about his injury—when his eye is caught. He straightens.

"Uh-oh," he says. "Looks like Mr. Koenig is here."

Utta Benrath had dark orange hair, strongly hennaed, which, with her green eyes, made her look foreign to Gudrun, but excitingly so. As if she were a half-breed of some impossible sort—Irish and Malay, Swedish and Peruvian. She was small and wiry and used her hands expressively when she spoke, fists unclenching slowly like a flower opening, or thrusting, palming movements, her fingers always flexing. Her voice was deep and she had a throaty, man's chuckle, like a hint of wicked fun. Gudrun met her when she had answered the advertisement Utta had placed on the notice board in the students' canteen: "Room to rent, share facilities and expenses."

When Gudrun began her affair with Tobias she realized she had to move out of the hostel she was staying in. The room in Utta's apartment was cheap and not just because the apartment was small and had no bathroom: it was inconvenient as well. Utta, it turned out, lived a brisk forty-five-minute walk from the Institute. The apartment was on the top floor of a tenement building on Grenz Weg, out in Jonitz, with a distant view of a turgid loop of the Mulde from the kitchen window. The place was clean and simply furnished. On the walls hung brightly colored designs for stained-glass windows that Utta had drawn in Weimar. Here in Dessau she was an assistant in the mural-painting workshop. She was older than Gudrun, in her early thirties, Gudrun guessed, but her unusual coloring made her age seem almost an irrelevance: she looked so unlike anyone Gudrun had seen before that age seemed to have little or nothing to do with the impression she made.

There were two bedrooms in the apartment on Grenz Weg, a small kitchen with a stove and a surprisingly generous hall where Utta and Gudrun would eat their meals around a square scrubbed pine table. They washed in the kitchen, standing on a towel in front of the sink. They carried their chamber pots down four flights of stairs and emptied them in the night-soil cistern at the rear of the small yard behind the

apartment building. Gudrun developed a strong affection for
their four rooms: her bedroom was the first of her own outside of her parents' house. It was the first proper home of her
adult life. Most evenings, she and Utta prepared their meal—
sausage, nine times out of ten, with potatoes or turnips—and
then, if they were not going out, they would sit on the bed in
Utta's room and listen to music on her phonograph. Utta
would read or write—she was studying architecture by corre-
spondence course—and they would talk. Utta's concentration, Gudrun soon noticed, her need for further credentials,
her ambitions, were motivated by a pessimistic obsession
about her position at the Institute, to which the conversation
inevitably returned. She told Gudrun she was convinced that
the mural-painting workshop was to be closed and she would
have to leave. She adduced evidence, clues, hints that she was
sure proved that this was Meyer's intention. Look what had
happened to stained glass, she said, to the wood- and stone-
carving workshops. The struggle it had been to transfer had
almost finished her off. That's why she wanted to be an architect: everything had to be practical these days, manufactured.
Productivity was the new God. But it took so long, and if they
closed the mural-painting workshop . . . Nothing Gudrun
said could reassure her. All Utta's energies were devoted to
finding a way to stay on.

"I've heard that Marianne Brandt hates Meyer," she re-
ported one night, with excitement, almost glee. "No, I mean
really hates him. She detests him. She's going to resign, I
know it."

"Maybe Meyer will go first," Gudrun said. "He's so unpop-
ular. It can't be nice for him."

Utta laughed. And laughed again. "Sweet Gudrun," she
said, and reached out and patted her foot. "Never change."

"But why should it affect you?" Gudrun asked. "Marianne
runs the metal workshop."

"Exactly," Utta said, with a small smile. "Don't you see? That means there'll be a vacancy, won't there?"

Mr. Koenig steps out of his car and wrinkles his eyes at the sun. Mrs. Koenig waits patiently until he comes around and opens the door for her. Everyone shakes hands.

"Bet you're glad you're not in Okinawa, eh, Spence?" Mr. Koenig says.

"Fire from heaven, I hear," Spencer says with some emotion.

"Oh yeah? Well, whatever." Mr. Koenig turns to me. "How're we doing, Miss Velk?"

"Running a bit late," I say. "Maybe in one hour, if you come back?"

He looks at his watch, then at his wife. "What do you say to some breakfast, Mrs. Koenig?"

Tobias liked to be naked. He liked to move around his house doing ordinary things, naked. Once when his wife was away he had cooked Gudrun a meal and asked her to eat it with him, naked. They ate thick slices of smoked ham, she remembered, with a pungent radish sauce. They sat in his dining room and ate and chatted as if all were perfectly normal. Gudrun realized that it aroused him sexually, that it was a prelude to lovemaking, but she began to feel cold and before he served the salad she asked if she could go and put on her sweater.

Tobias Henzi was one of the three Masters of Form who ran the architecture workshop. He was a big burly man who would become seriously fat in a few years, Gudrun realized. His body was covered with a pelt of fine dark hair, almost like an animal's, it grew thickly on his chest and belly and, curiously, in the small of his back, but his whole body—his buttocks, his shoulders—was covered with this fine glossy fur. At first she thought she would find it repugnant, but it was soft, not wiry, and now when they were in bed she often discovered herself absentmindedly stroking him, as if he were a great cat or a bear, as if he were a rug she could pull around her.

They met at the New Year's party in 1928, where the theme was "white." Tobias had gone as a grotesque, padded Pierrot, a white cone on his head, his face a mask of white greasepaint. Gudrun had been a colonialist, in a man's white suit with a white shirt and tie and her hair up under a solar topee. By the party's end, well into January 1, she had gone into an upstairs lavatory to untie her tight bun, vaguely hoping that loosening her hair would ease her headache.

Her hair was longer then, falling to her shoulders, and as she came down the stairs to the main hall she saw, sitting on a landing, Tobias, a large, rumpled, clearly drunken Pierrot, smoking a dark knobbled cigar. He watched her descend, a little amazed, it seemed, blinking as if to clear some obstruction to his vision.

She stepped over his leg, she knew who he was.

"Hey, you," he shouted after her. "I didn't know you were a woman." His tone was affronted, aggressive, almost as if she had deliberately misled him. She did not look around.

The day the new term began he came to the weaving workshop to find her.

I take my last cigarette from the pack and light it. I sit on the step below the cab of Spencer's crane, where there's some shade. I see Spencer coming briskly along the sidewalk from the pay phone. He's a stocky man, not small, but with the stocky man's vigorous rolling stride, as if the air were crowding him and he's shouldering it away, forcing his passage through.

"They say it left an hour ago." He shrugged. "Must be some problem on the highway."

"Wonderful." I blow smoke into the sky, loudly, to show my exasperation.

"Can I bum one of those off of you?"

I show him the empty pack.

"Lucky Strike." He shrugs. "I don't like them, anyway."

"I like the name. That's why I smoke them."

He looks at me. "Yeah, where do they get the names for those packs? Who makes them up? I ask you."

"Camel."

"Yeah," he says. "Why a camel? Do camels smoke? Why not a . . . a hippo? I ask you."

I laugh. "A pack of Hippos, please."

He grins and cuffs the headlamp nacelle. He makes a *tsssss* sound, and shakes his head, incredulously. He looks back at me.

"Goddamn factory. Must be something on the highway."

"Can I buy you some breakfast, Spencer?"

Paul met Tobias only once in Gudrun's company. It was one afternoon at four o'clock when the workshops closed. The weavers worked four hours in the morning, two in the afternoon. The workshop was empty. The big rug was half done, pinned up on an easel in the middle of the room. Paul stood in front of it, the fingers of his right hand slowly stroking his chin, looking, thinking. From time to time he would cover his left eye with his left palm.

"I like it, Gudrun," he said, finally. "I like its warmth and clarity. The color penetration, the orangy pinks, the lemons . . . What's going to happen at the bottom?"

"I think I am going to shade into green and blue."

"What's that black?"

"I'm going to have some bars, some vertical, one horizontal, with the cold colors."

He nodded and stepped back. Gudrun, who had been standing behind him, moved to one side to allow him a longer view. As she turned, she saw Tobias had come into the room and was watching them. Tobias sauntered over and greeted Paul coolly and with formality.

"I came to admire the rug," Paul said. "It's splendid, no?"

Tobias glanced at it. "Very decorative," he said. "You should be designing wallpaper, Miss Velk, not wasting your time with this." He turned to Paul. "Don't you agree?"

"Ah. Popular necessities before elitist luxuries," Paul said, wagging a warning finger at her, briefly. The sarcasm sounded most strange coming from him, Gudrun thought.

"It's a way of putting it," Tobias said. "Indeed."

We sit in a window of a coffee shop in Westwood Village. I've ordered a coffee and Danish but Spencer has decided to go for something more substantial: a rib-eye steak with fried egg.

"I hope the Koenigs don't come back," Spencer says. "Maybe I shouldn't have ordered the steak."

I press my cheek against the warm glass of the window. I can just see the back end of Spencer's crane.

"I'll spot them," I say. "And I'll see the truck from the factory. You eat up."

Spencer runs his finger along the curved aluminum beading that finishes the table edge.

"I want you to know, Miss Velk, how grateful I am for the work you've put my way." He looks me in the eye. "More than grateful."

"No, it is I who am grateful to you."

"No, no, I appreciate what you—"

His steak comes and puts an end to what I'm sure would have been long protestations of mutual gratitude. It's too hot to eat pastry so I push my Danish aside and wonder where I can buy some more cigarettes. Spencer, holding his fork like a dagger in his injured left hand, stabs it into his steak to keep it steady on the plate and, with the knife in his right, sets about trying to saw the meat into pieces. He is having difficulty: his thumb and two fingers can't keep a good grip on the fork handle, and he saws with the knife awkwardly.

"Damn thing is I'm left-handed," he says, sensing me watching. He works off a small corner, pops it in his mouth and then starts the whole pinioning, slicing operation again. The plate slides across the shiny tabletop and collides with my coffee mug. A small splash flips out.

"Sorry," he says.

"Could I do that for you?" I say. "Would it bother you?"

He says nothing and I reach out and gently take the knife and fork from him. I cut the steak into cubes and hand back the knife and fork.

"Thank you, Miss Velk."

"Please call me Gudrun," I say.

"Thank you, Gudrun."

"Gudrun! Gudrun, over here." Utta beckoned her from the doorway of Tobias's kitchen. Gudrun moved with difficulty through the crowd of people, finding a gap here, skirting around an expansive gesture there. Utta drew her into the kitchen, where there was still quite a mob of people, and re-filled Gudrun's glass with punch and then her own. They clinked glasses.

"I give you Marianne Brandt," Utta said. She smiled.

"What do you mean?"

"She's resigned."

"What happened? Who told you?"

Utta inclined her head toward the window. "Irene," she said. Standing by the sink talking to three young men was Irene Henzi, Tobias's wife. Gudrun had not seen her there. She had arrived at the party late, uneasy at the thought of being in Tobias's house, meeting his wife and other guests. Tobias had assured her that Irene knew nothing; Irene was ignorance personified, he said, the quintessence of ignorance. Utta carried on talking, as Gudrun covertly scrutinized her hostess, hearing some business about amalgamation, about metal, joinery and mural painting all being coordinated into a new workshop of interior design. Irene did not look like an ignorant woman, she thought, she looked like a woman brimful of knowledge. "—I told you it would happen. Arndt's going to run it. But Marianne's refused to continue," Utta was saying, but Gudrun did not listen further. Irene Henzi was tall and thin, she had a sharp long face with hooded, sleepy eyes and wore a loose black gown that seemed oddly Eastern in design. To Gudrun she appeared almost ugly, and yet she seemed to have gathered within her a languid, self-confident calm and serenity. The students laughed at something she said, and she left them with a flick of her wrist, making them laugh again, picking up a plate of canapés and beginning to offer them around to the other guests standing and chatting in the kitchen. She drifted toward Utta and Gudrun, closer, a smile and word for everyone.

"I have to go," Gudrun said, and left.

Utta caught up with her in the hall, where she was putting on her coat.

"What's happening? Where are you going?"

"Home. I don't feel well."

"But I want you to talk to Tobias, find out more. They need a new assistant now. If Tobias could mention my name to Meyer, just a mention . . ."

Gudrun felt a genuine nausea and simultaneously, inexplicably, infuriatingly, an urge to cry.

Spencer frowns worriedly at me. I look at my watch, Mr. Koenig looks at his watch also and simultaneously the truck from the factory in Oxnard rumbles up Wilshire. Apologies are offered, the delays on the highway blamed—who would have thought there could be so much traffic on a Sunday?— and Spencer maneuvers the crane into position.

Tobias ran his fingertips down her back to the cleft in her buttocks. "So smooth," he said. He turned her over and nuzzled her breasts, taking her hand and pulling it down to his groin.

"Utta will be home soon," she said.

Tobias groaned. He heaved himself up on his elbows and looked down at her. "I can't stand this," he said. "You have to get a place of your own. And not so damn far away."

"Oh yes, of course," Gudrun said. "I'll get a little apartment on Kavalierstrasse. So convenient and so reasonable."

"I'm going to miss you," he said. "What am I going to do? Dear Christ."

Gudrun had told him she was going to take the dyeing course at Sorau. They met regularly now, almost as a matter of routine, three, sometimes four times a week in the afternoon at the apartment on Grenz Weg. The weaving workshop closed earlier than the other departments in the Institute, and between half past four and half past six in the afternoons they had the flat to themselves. Utta would obligingly stop for a coffee or shop on her way home—dawdling for the sake of love, as she described it—and usually Tobias was gone by the time she returned. On the occasions they met he seemed quite indifferent, quite unperturbed at being seen.

"Now, if Utta was the new head of the metal workshop," Gudrun said, "I'm sure she'd be much more busy than—"

"Don't start that again," Tobias said. "I've spoken to Meyer. Arndt has his own candidates. You know she has a fair chance. A more than fair chance." He put his arms around her and squeezed her strongly to him. "Gudrun, my Gudrun," he exclaimed, as if mystified by this emotion within him. "Why do I want you so? Why?"

They heard the rattle of Utta's key in the lock, her steps as she crossed the hall into the kitchen.

When Tobias left, Utta came immediately to Gudrun's room. She was dressing, but the bed was still a mess of rumpled sheets, which for some reason made Gudrun embarrassed. To her the room seemed to reek of Tobias. She pulled the blanket up to the pillow.

"Did he see you when he left?" Gudrun asked.

"No, I was in my room. Did he say anything?"

"The same as usual. No, 'a more than fair chance,' he said. He said Arndt has his own candidates."

"Of course, but 'a more than fair chance.' That's something. Yes . . ."

"Utta, I can't do anything more. I think I should stop asking. Why don't you see Meyer yourself?"

"No, no. It's not the way it works here, you don't understand. It never has. You have to play it differently. And you must never give up."

Spencer checks that the canvas webbing is properly secured under the base, jumps down from the truck and climbs up to the small control platform beside the crane.

I remind Mr. Koenig: "It's manufactured in three parts. The whole thing can be assembled quickly. It's painted, finished. We connect the power supply and you're in business."

Mr. Koenig was visibly moved. "It's incredible," he said. "Just like that."

I turn to Spencer and give him a thumbs-up. There's a thin puff of bluey-gray smoke and the crane's motor chugs into life.

Tobias sat on the edge of his desk, one leg swinging. He reached out to take Gudrun's hand and gently pulled her into the V of his thighs. He kissed her neck and inhaled, smelling her skin, her hair, as if he were trying to draw her essence deep into his lungs.

"I want us to go away for a weekend," he said. "Let's go to Berlin."

She kissed him. "I can't afford it."

"I'll pay," he said. "I'll think of something, some crucial meeting."

She felt his hands on her buttocks; his thighs gently clamped hers. Through the wall of his office she could hear male voices from one of the drawing rooms. She pushed herself away from him and strolled over to the tilted drawing table that was set before the window.

"A weekend in Berlin . . ." she said. "I like the sound of that, I must—"

She turned as the door opened and Irene Henzi walked in.

"Tobias, we're late," she said, glancing at Gudrun with a faint smile.

Tobias sat on, one free leg swinging slightly.

"You know Miss Velk, don't you?"

"I don't think so. How are you?"

Somehow Gudrun managed to extend her arm; she felt the slight pressure of dry cool fingers. "A pleasure."

"She was at the party," Tobias said. "Surely you met."

"Darling, there were a hundred people at the party."

"I won't disturb you further," Gudrun said, moving to the door. "Very good to meet you."

"Oh, Miss Velk." Tobias's call stopped her; she turned carefully to see Irene bent over the drawing table scrutinizing the blueprint there. "Don't forget our appointment. Four-thirty as usual." He smiled at her, glanced over to make sure his wife was not observing and blew her a kiss.

At the edge of a wood of silver birches behind the Institute was a small meadow where, in summer, the students would go and sunbathe. And at the meadow's edge a stream ran, thick with willows and alders. The pastoral mood was regularly dispelled, however—and Gudrun wondered if this was why it was so popular with students—by the roaring noise of aeroengines. The trimotors that were tested at the Junkers Flugplatz, just beyond the pine trees to the west, would bank around and fly low over the meadow as they made their landing approaches. In the summer the pilots would wave to the sunbathing students below.

Gudrun walked down the path through the birchwood, still trembling, still hot from the memory of Tobias's audacity, his huge composure. She was surprised to see, coming up from the meadow, Paul. He was carrying a pair of binoculars in his hand. He saw her and waved.

"I like to look at the aeroplanes," he said. "In the war I used to work at an airfield, you know, painting camouflage. Wonderful machines."

She had a flask of coffee with her and spontaneously offered to share it with him. She needed some company, she felt, some genial distraction. They found a place by the stream and she poured coffee into the tin cup that doubled as the flask's top. She had some bread and two hard-boiled eggs, which she ate as Paul drank the coffee. Then he filled his pipe and smoked while she told him about the dyeing course at Sorau. He said he thought she needed a more intense blue to finish her rug, something hard and metallic, and suggested she might be able to concoct the right color at the dye works.

"With Tobias," he said suddenly, to her surprise, "when you're with Tobias, are you happy?"

He waved aside her denials and queries. Everyone knew about it, he told her, such a thing could not be done discreetly in a place like the Institute. She need not answer if she did not want to, but he was curious.

Yes, she said, she was very happy with Tobias. They were both happy. She said boldly that she thought she was in love with him. Paul listened. He told her that Tobias was a powerful figure in the architecture school, that all power in the Institute emanated from the architecture workshop. He would not be surprised, he said, if one day Tobias ended up running the whole place.

He rose to his feet, tapped out his pipe on the trunk of a willow and they wandered back through the birchwood.

"I just wanted you to be aware about this," he said, "about Tobias." He smiled at her. "He's an intriguing man." His features were small beneath his wide pale brow, as if crushed and squashed slightly by its weight. There were bags under his eyes, she noticed, he looked tired.

"You're like a meteor," he said. "Suddenly you're attracted by the earth and are drawn into its atmosphere. At this moment you become a shooting star, incandescent and beautiful. There are two options available: to be tied to the earth's atmosphere and plummet, or to escape, moving back out into space—"

She was baffled at first, but then remembered he was quoting from his own courses, something she had heard in his classes.

"—where you slowly cool down and eventually extinguish. The point is you need not plummet," he said carefully.

"There are different laws in different atmospheres, freer movements, freer dynamics. It need not be rigid."

"Loose continuity," she said. "I remember."

"Precisely," he said with a smile. "There's a choice. Rigid or loose continuity." He tapped her arm lightly. "Do you know, I think I may be interested in buying your rug."

Spencer tightens the final bolt and crosses the street to join us on the opposite sidewalk. Mr. Koenig, Mrs. Koenig, Spencer and me. It is almost midday, and the sun is almost insupportably bright. I put on my sunglasses and through their green glass I stare at the Koenigs' mini-diner.

Mr. Koenig turns away and takes a few paces, his finger held under his nose as if he were about to sneeze. He comes back to us.

"I love it, Miss Velk," he says after apologizing for the few private moments he has needed. "I just . . . It's so . . . The way you've done those jutting-out bits. My God, it even looks like a sandwich. The roll, the meat . . . So clever, so new. How it curves like that, that style—"

"Streamline moderne, we call it."

"May I?"

He puts his hands on my shoulders and leans forward and up (I am a little taller) and he gives me a swift kiss on the cheek.

"I don't normally kiss architects—"

"Oh, I'm not an architect," I say. "I'm just a designer. It was a challenge."

Gudrun never really knew what happened (but this is what I think, I'm sure it was like this), as the stories changed so often in the telling, and there were lies and half-lies all the time.

The truth made both guilty parties more guilty and they thought to absolve themselves by pleading spontaneity, and helpless instinct, but they had no time to compare notes and the discrepancies hinted at quite another version of reality.

Gudrun climbed the last block from the station and quietly opened the door of the apartment on Grenz Weg. It must have been a little before eight o'clock in the morning. She had gone a few steps into the hall when she heard a sound in the kitchen. She pushed open the door and Tobias stood there, naked, with two cups of steaming coffee in his hands.

His look of awful incomprehension changing to awful comprehension lasted no more than a second. He smiled, set down the cups, said "Gudrun—" and was interrupted by Utta's call from her bedroom. "Tobias, where's that coffee, for heaven's sake?"

Gudrun (to this day) doesn't know why she did what she did. She picked up a coffee cup and walked into Utta's room. She wanted Utta to see that there was to be no evasion of responsibility. Utta was sitting up in her bed, pillows plumped behind her, the sheet to her waist. Tobias's clothes were piled untidily on a wooden chair. She made a kind of sick, choking noise when Gudrun came in. For a moment Gudrun thought of throwing the hot coffee at her, but at that stage she knew there were only seconds before she herself would break, so, after a moment of standing there to make Utta see, to make her know, she dropped the cup on the floor and left the apartment.

Two days later Tobias asked Gudrun to marry him. He said he had gone to the apartment on Saturday night (his wife was away) thinking that was the day she was returning from Sorau. Why would he think that? she asked, they had talked about a Sunday reunion so many times. Once in his stream of protestations he had inadvertently referred to a note—"I mean, what would you think? a note like that"—and then, when questioned—"What note? Who sent you a note?"—said he was becoming confused—no, there was no note, he had meant to say she *should* have sent him a note from Sorau, not relied on him to remember, how could he remember everything, for God's sweet sake?

Utta. Utta had written to him, Gudrun surmised, perhaps in her name, the better to lure him: "Darling Tobias, I'm coming home a day early, meet me at the apartment on Saturday night. Your own Gudrun . . ." It would work easily. Utta there, surprised to see him. Come in, sit down, now you're here, come all this way. Something to drink, some wine, some schnapps, maybe? And Tobias's vanity, Tobias's opportunism and Tobias's weakness would do the rest. Now, darling, Tobias, this question of Marianne Brandt's resignation . . .

In weary moments, though, other possibilities presented themselves to her. Older duplicities, histories and motives she could never have known about and wouldn't want to contemplate. Her own theory was easier to live with.

Utta wrote her a letter: ". . . no idea how it happened . . . some madness that can infect us all . . . an act of no meaning, of momentary release." She was sad to lose Utta as a friend, but not so sad to turn down Tobias's proposal of marriage.

I say goodbye to Spencer as he sits in the cab of his crane looking down at me. "See you tomorrow, Gudrun," he says with a smile, to my vague surprise, until I remember I had asked him to call me Gudrun. He drives away and I rejoin Mr. Koenig.

"I got one question," he says. "I mean, I love the lettering, don't get me wrong—'sandwiches, salads, hot dogs'—but why no capital letters?"

"Well," I say without thinking, "why write with capitals when we don't speak with capitals?"

Mr. Koenig frowns. "What? . . . Yeah, it's a fair point. Never thought of it that way . . . Yeah."

My mind begins to wander again, as Mr. Koenig starts to put a proposition to me. Who said that about typography? Was it Albers? Paul? . . . No, Moholy-Nagy. László in his red overalls with his lumpy boxer's face and his intellectual's spectacles. He is in Chicago now. We're all gone, I think to myself, all scattered.

Mr. Koenig is telling me that there are fifteen Koenig mini-diners in the Los Angeles area and he would like, he hopes, he wonders if it would be possible for me to redesign them—all of them—in this streamline, modern streamline sort of style.

All scattered. Freer. Freer movements, freer dynamics. I remember, and smile to myself. I had never imagined a future designing hot dog stands in a city on the West Coast of America. It is a kind of continuity, I suppose. We need not plummet. Paul would approve of me and what I have done, I think, as a vindication of his principle.

I hear myself accepting Mr. Koenig's offer and allow him to kiss me on the cheek once more—but my mind is off once again, a continent and an ocean away in drab and misty Dessau. Gudrun Velk is trudging up the gentle slope of Grillparzerstrasse, her suitcase heavy in her hand, taking the shortcut from the station, heading back to the small apartment on Grenz Weg which she shares with her friend Utta Benrath and hoping, wondering, now that she has managed to catch an early train from Sorau, if Tobias would have some time to see her alone that afternoon.

A NOTE ON THE TYPE

This book was set in Janson, a typeface long thought to have been made by the Dutchman Anton Janson, who was a practicing typefounder in Leipzig during the years 1668–1687. However, it has been conclusively demonstrated that these types are actually the work of Nicholas Kis (1650–1702), a Hungarian, who most probably learned his trade from the master Dutch typefounder Dirk Voskens. The type is an excellent example of the influential and sturdy Dutch types that prevailed in England up to the time William Caslon (1692–1766) developed his own incomparable designs from them.

Composed by PennSet, Inc.,
Bloomsburg, Pennsylvania

Printed and bound by Quebecor Printing,
Fairfield, Pennsylvania

Designed by Cassandra J. Pappas